SILENCED

"I can't let you or anyone else find out . . ."

A kitchen knife appeared from inside the jacket.

She stepped backward and shrieked, "You can't just kill a person for . . ."

The fist holding the knife shot forward and she didn't have a chance to move aside. A searing pain rushed through her body. As her knees buckled, a soft whimper escaped her lips. The room spun, flew out of focus, then turned black.

She felt herself hit the floor, then the heaviness of the pain left her body. Footsteps moved slowly away from her. She heard a door creak, then creak again . . . and then only silence.

Avon Books are available at special quantity discounts for bulk purchases for sales promotions, premiums, fund raising or educational use. Special books, or book excerpts, can also be created to fit specific needs.

For details write or telephone the office of the Director of Special Markets, Avon Books, Dept. FP, 1350 Avenue of the Americas, New York, New York 10019, 1-800-238-0658.

Crash Landing

NICOLE DAVIDSON

AN AVON FLARE BOOK

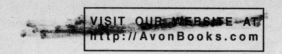

VISIT OUR WEBSITE AT
http://AvonBooks.com

CRASH LANDING is an original publication of Avon Books. This work has never before appeared in book form.

AVON BOOKS
A division of
The Hearst Corporation
1350 Avenue of the Americas
New York, New York 10019

Copyright © 1996 by Kathryn Jensen
Published by arrangement with the author
Library of Congress Catalog Card Number: 96-96183
ISBN: 0-380-78153-0
RL: 5.5

First Avon Flare Printing: October 1996

AVON FLARE TRADEMARK REG. U.S. PAT. OFF. AND IN OTHER COUNTRIES, MARCA REGISTRADA, HECHO EN U.S.A.

Printed in the U.S.A.

RA   10   9   8   7   6   5   4   3   2

1

She hadn't wanted to come here ever again.

Kelly Ann Peterson stood at the frozen edge of Deep Creek Lake, tears trickling down the hollows of her cheeks. Before she could lift her mittened hands to brush the moisture away, it solidified in salty trails on her skin.

"Brian. Oh Brian . . . no!" a strangled sob gushed from her throat.

That night came back to her in too-vivid flashes—like a scene acted out on an MTV video under pulsating strobe lights. Screams from the dark woods. The frenzied search. The horrible realization that Brian had drowned in the murky waters of the lake at the foot of Wisp Mountain.

Painful memories dragged her back down to a place she'd struggled to escape for over a year. The terrible depression that had seized Kelly after her best friend's death settled over her again like a suffocating blanket of snow.

As the March wind sliced down Wisp, chilling Kelly to the bone, a twig snapped behind her. She jumped and spun around.

Annette Riley, Thomaston High's ski club advisor, stepped out of the woods. She was wearing a one-piece ski suit—vivid purple and green splashes of color against the snow-covered landscape. Her cheeks were a pretty pink from the cold.

Kelly wished Annette would just go away and leave her alone.

Alone with her memories and with the hurt.

"Are you all right, Kelly?" Annette asked, stopping beside her. She laid a hand on her arm.

The young teacher looked not much older than many of her students. They all called her by her first name, unless the principal, Mr. Corning, was in earshot. She'd been voted the most way-cool teacher at Thomaston High for this year's yearbook.

"I'll be okay . . . in a minute," Kelly said, blotting at her eyes again.

"Jeff said you might be here. What's so special about this spot?"

Jeff Mitchell was her boyfriend. He was the one good thing that had come out of her last trip to the lake.

Kelly couldn't answer. Her throat closed around a tennis ball–size lump. Looking out across the lake, she shook her head.

This winter had been an especially cold one for western Maryland. Arctic blasts from Canada tore across the mountainous ridges, dumping tons of snow throughout January and February. Even folks far to the east in Baltimore, where the seasons were milder, joked about another Ice Age coming.

The frigid temps didn't seem to want to let up even now, in March, when the spring thaw usually came. The only people happy with the weather were the ski resort employees and skiers themselves, who rejoiced in the unusually long season.

Kelly had been skiing for years, and she loved the sport. But the incident at the lake that November had changed her life in ways she could never have predicted.

"Kelly, I can't let you stay out here alone,"

Annette said softly. "Please come back to the lodge with me."

Kelly shook her head. Red curls tumbled into her eyes, but she ignored them.

"Why not? What's so important about this place? Tell me. You'll feel better."

Kelly turned to face the teacher. "You really don't know? No one told you?"

Annette looked puzzled. "No. Jeff said something about letting you tell me. Maybe he thinks talking about it would be good for you."

The last thing in the world Kelly wanted to do was relive that Thanksgiving vacation. But from somewhere deep inside of her a need bubbled up, like a kettle coming to a slow boil. She would tell the story.

Kelly brushed the snow off of a boulder and sat down heavily, pulling her knees up to her chin with her arms. The layers of thermal underwear, turtleneck jersey, and down-filled parka did nothing to warm her. She blocked out the cold, willing herself beyond the aching brittleness in her fingers and toes.

"I-I don't know how to begin," she whispered.

"Begin with the reason you're so unhappy here. When the ski club planned to go to Vermont over spring break, you were excited about the trip," Annette said, perching beside her on the rock. "When we didn't have enough money to travel that far, Wisp seemed to be the best alternative."

"It's not Wisp that bothers me," Kelly explained. "It's not the mountain, it's the lake." She swallowed. Her eyes were burning again, but she fought back a new wave of tears.

"What about the lake?"

"My very best friend Brian Lopez drowned here, a little over a year ago."

Annette draped an arm over her shoulders. "I'm sorry. I really didn't know. Why didn't you or one of the other kids say something to me before I made the plans?"

Kelly shrugged. "Some of them don't know. And Will wanted to come to Wisp really bad. The others probably didn't connect it with Deep Creek. I knew. I tried to talk everyone into sticking with the Vermont plan. Remember how we took a vote?"

"The others voted you down."

"Yeah."

Annette shook her head. "If I'd realized . . . How did it happen?" Then she must have seen the stricken look on Kelly's face. "Never mind," she said quickly. "That was a thoughtless question."

"It's all right," Kelly said. "I want to talk about it now. I need to remember. For Brian . . ."

Kelly took her time, starting at the very beginning of that other school trip, explaining who had come and what had happened. Annette didn't interrupt once.

The trip had been arranged as a special crash course to bone up for the SATs. A handful of students who were worried about their scores had signed up—or were enrolled by their parents—including Kelly, Jeff Mitchell, Brian Lopez, Brian's girlfriend Paula Schultz, and a few other kids. There was Nathan, a social dropout; Angel, a morose girl who always dressed in black; Chris, a jock who'd become addicted to taking steroids as a body-building aid; and Isabel, whose grandfather was a Navaho Indian. She'd helped Chris kick the steroids.

Their first night at the lake, even before they'd gotten to know one another, there'd been a terrible accident. Brian had drowned, and no one knew why or how.

Kelly had been determined to find the person responsible. She'd nearly lost her own life uncovering the truth.

"It turned out that Paula was so upset when she realized she and Brian would have to be apart when they went to college, she started fantasizing about a suicide pact," Kelly explained.

"Oh, no," Annette murmured.

Kelly nodded sadly. "I guess, to Paula, the idea seemed romantic—lovers forever together at the bottom of Deep Creek Lake. No one could take Brian away from her then. But Brian knew it was wrong and, apparently, he refused to go along with her plan. Paula kept after him. She wouldn't drop the idea, and at last Brian came up with a plan to shock Paula back to her senses."

"I take it something went wrong," Annette said.

"Yes." Kelly swallowed and let her eyes take her out across the frozen, snow-covered lake. "Brian waited until dark then took Paula in a rowboat, out into the middle of the lake. He pretended he was going to do it . . . he was going to jump in. He'd even loaded rocks into their pockets, saying they'd sink faster that way.

"I think he expected that once he got her out there she'd beg for him to take her back to shore. But she panicked and the boat rocked and Bri fell in and . . . and he drowned."

"I'm sorry," Annette said.

Kelly squeezed her eyes shut; she could feel her pulse throbbing behind her eyelids. "Paula must have been terrified she'd be blamed for Brian's death," Kelly continued. "She did everything she could to keep what had really happened a secret. She invented a mysterious attacker. When Nathan figured out she was lying, she tried to kill him. She nearly killed me too." Kelly opened her eyes, clenching her fists at her sides. "I've never hated

5

anyone as much as I hated Paula when I realized what she'd done."

"Hate doesn't solve anything," Annette said.

"Sometimes it's easier to let yourself hate than to hurt so much inside," Kelly murmured, suddenly exhausted.

She hadn't been skiing for over a year, not since the last time she and Brian had driven up to Pennsylvania to ski with her dad. In fact, she hadn't done much in the way of any kind of exercise. She felt too tired most of the time.

Annette said, "What happened to Paula?"

"At first the police said she'd be tried for Brian's murder and the attempted murder of me and Nathan."

"The same Nathan who's with us on this trip?"

Kelly nodded. "But her parents hired a team of psychiatrists who examined her. The doctors wrote a letter to the judge, saying Paula was mentally ill and she was incapable of standing trial. The court turned her over to a special psychiatric hospital for long-term treatment."

"She's still there?"

"Yeah."

The icy wind grated through the tall evergreen trees, rattling dry, pine-scented needles overhead. Kelly wrapped her arms around her ribs and shivered.

"I'm so sorry," Annette said apologetically. "We could have gone to another resort. White Tail would have been fine. It's closer to Thomaston and cheaper."

"Everyone else was so excited about coming here. Anyway, my dad says I have to face the facts sooner or later."

Annette boosted herself to her feet and pulled Kelly up after her. "Still, it's your life. Only *you* know what's the right decision for you."

Kelly glanced across at the young teacher as they walked back through the woods, then across the street and toward the lodge at the base of Wisp. Had she imagined the catch in her voice? Annette's eyes looked misted over, and the muscles were pulled tensely across the bones of her face, as if something more than Kelly's dark mood was worrying her.

Only you know what's the right decision . . . Had Annette made a decision of her own that she regretted?

Kelly decided it was none of her business. She kept on walking in silence.

They were almost back to the lodge when two figures on cross-country skis approached from the other direction. Kelly smiled at Jeff's familiar black ski jacket and yellow-tinted goggles. Striding awkwardly along beside him was Nathan. The other boy looked miserable. His skin was an unhealthy gray against the snow, and he was moving sluggishly, as if only half awake.

"Hey look!" Jeff cried. "Two beautiful snow bunnies!"

"I thought you two were taking another run down Possum Way," Kelly called out, forcing herself to sound cheerful. She didn't want Jeff to know she'd been crying.

"We did, but when we got back to the cabin, Frank sent us out to look for you two."

Frank Riley was Annette's husband.

"He worries too much," Annette commented.

"Why'd he bother coming at all?" Nathan grumbled. "He can't ski, and he's done nothing but complain the whole trip."

Kelly gave Nathan a sharp look, afraid he'd hurt Annette's feelings. But the teacher seemed not to have heard him.

Jeff laughed. "Like you, Mr. Optimism, never complain?"

"Well, it don't make sense to me," Nathan continued, ignoring Kelly's warning glare. "I mean, like Frank can't even ride the chairlifts to the top. The only way to get him up the mountain is if someone drives him up the back roads or—"

"Shut up, Nathan," Jeff snapped.

Kelly felt bad for Frank Riley. He had been seriously injured in a skiing accident while he and Annette had been in college. He'd survived but was paralyzed below the waist. The doctors said he'd never walk again. But he zoomed around town in a specially equipped Jeep and in his ultralight wheelchair. He'd even raced in the Marine Corps marathon in Washington, D.C., and he played basketball in a wheelchair league. Unfortunately, there were things he couldn't handle as well. Snow was one of them.

"Maybe Frank just wanted to keep Annette company," Kelly said, and Annette met her eyes with a soft smile. "I think that's very romantic."

Nathan snorted his disgust.

"Look," Jeff said, pointing through the trees as if glad of a distraction, "here come some of the others."

Four high school students, carrying skis over their shoulders, plodded through the trees in molded plastic ski boots that looked like footwear fashioned for lunar explorers. They were laughing and breathing hard, thumping with exaggerated clumsiness across the snow.

Will Tanner, who had come to Thomaston High in October of that school year, led the way. Kelly didn't know him very well, but all the junior and senior girls considered him a massive hunk. He drove a cool car and got invited to every party for miles around.

Behind him trailed Angel. Then Isabel and Chris.

Kelly couldn't help thinking about how much her friends had changed in just one year.

Angel had once worn only black, and spoke constantly about doom and destruction. She'd been the spookiest girl Kelly had ever known. But a few weeks after Brian's death, she showed up at school wearing a long white dress. Her black hair had been bleached a silvery gold, and she told Kelly she'd been visited by a bevy of her namesakes . . . *real angels*. In some ways, the new Angel was creepier than the old one.

Isabel and Chris were still hanging together. Chris had stopped taking steroids after a lot of encouragement from Isabel. He was no longer violent or moody, and he seemed to be better able to concentrate on the plays during a game and on his schoolwork. His size and strength were a little less intimidating, but he was still the toughest player on Thomaston's varsity team.

Isabel was prettier than ever with her soft mocha skin and long, dark hair. She and Kelly had become close friends during the past year. But even her comforting words couldn't make Kelly let go of the hate that burned inside of her for Paula Schultz. Paula, who'd cost Brian his life and had gotten away without punishment.

Kelly felt Jeff watching her, and she looked up out of her secret anger and forced her lips into a smile. "Are you done skiing for the day?" she asked.

"Naw, just ready for a break. Thought we could all grab something to eat at Pizzazz!" That was the local pizza and snack den, popular with the younger crowd. There was also a family-style restaurant called the Bavarian Room; Shenanigan's, a night club; and two pubs. "Then we can ski again tonight, under the lights."

Kelly felt her grim mood lighten. She grinned at Jeff. "You never get enough of the white stuff, do you?"

"I'm just getting the hang of this sport," Jeff laughed. "I'm not like you and Will, the pros."

Will socked him good-naturedly in the arm. "Hey, I'm not that good."

Annette rolled her eyes. "You're good enough to race competitively in college, if you took your skiing seriously."

"Not going to college," he informed her smugly. "Too much work."

"College isn't just studying books, you know," Annette pointed out. "Some of what you learn on a campus is about life, like how to be a better person."

Will shrugged. "Hey, why mess with perfection?"

Everyone laughed. Will's ego was famous.

They arrived together at the cabin Annette had rented for the week. Kelly knocked the snow off her boots before stepping into the cozy interior.

She was the first one through the door. She was the first one to see Frank Riley with the knife.

2

Jerking to a halt, Kelly stared at Annette's husband.

He was leaning forward in his wheelchair, clutching what appeared to be a kitchen knife in his left hand. The pupils of his eyes were tiny black pinpricks against two waxy gray orbs. They were riveted on two teenage boys whose backs were pressed against a wall.

"Hey, get this guy away from us!" the taller of the two boys shouted. "He's psycho!"

Annette burst through the door behind Kelly, pushing her aside. "Frank, what *on earth* are you doing?"

Her husband scooted his chair forward another few inches, closing the gap between himself and his cowering prey. "I found these two in one of the bedrooms, trying to steal stuff."

"We weren't . . . honest!" the smaller boy whimpered.

Annette snatched the knife out of Frank's hand. "Whether or not these kids were stealing is beside the point. You don't threaten people with dangerous weapons, you call the police."

"We don't have a phone," he stated. "They'd have gotten away." He looked deeply disappointed.

The rest of the ski club piled into the room behind Kelly. She squinted at the two strangers. They seemed to be about her age. The taller one was nice looking in an ordinary brown-hair, brown-eyes kind of way. He seemed to her to be one of those people who didn't stick in your mind. As soon as he left a room, people would have trouble remembering what he looked like . . . or even that he'd been there.

The other boy was trembling like a mouse whose tail is caught beneath a cat's paw. He had sandy-colored hair and wore old-fashioned spectacles with magnifying-glass lenses. She wondered how he managed to ski without them. Regular glasses always fogged up horribly and he'd be blind in goggles.

"Explain what you're doing in this cabin," Annette said, giving the boys her no-nonsense teacher-stare.

The tall boy stepped forward. "I'm Troy York. Listen, this is all my fault. I'm really sorry for causing you any trouble."

"*You* are the one with trouble on your hands," Frank chimed in. "When the cops get hold of you two—"

"Please, don't call the police," Troy said quickly. "We really didn't mean any harm."

"Harm, my foot!"

"Frank, shut up," Annette said. "Let the boy talk."

Troy cleared his throat, looking around the room at the circle of expectant faces. Kelly could tell he was nervous, but she didn't feel sorry for him. At the very least he deserved a good scare for breaking into someone's cabin.

"This is my friend Jeremy Potter," Troy began. Jeremy gave a stiff nod. "We're here from Randalls-town High, with our ski club—"

"Gee! Us too!" Angel cried, looking thrilled at the coincidence.

Troy blinked at Angel, as if for the first time noticing her—although she was hard to miss in her

12

blindingly white jumpsuit. "Yeah, well anyway . . . we went into the snack bar at lunchtime and left our skis and stuff outside. When we came back, Jeremy's goggles were gone."

"They have prescription lenses with a special ultraviolet tint," Jeremy explained meekly. He wiped his nose on the sleeve of his jacket, like a little kid. "It's not safe to ski without them."

"Did you check with lost and found in the lodge?" Kelly asked.

"We checked *everywhere*. Nothing. Niente. Nada." He looked with obvious interest at Kelly, and she smiled back at him, wondering if he was flirting or just being friendly.

"So you decided to take the investigation for the missing goggles into your own hands," Annette said.

Troy studied his feet, and strands of brown hair fell over his eyes. "Yeah. Guess that wasn't such a good idea."

"Guess not," Frank snapped.

Annette shot him a look that seemed to say she'd take care of the situation. Glumly, he wheeled himself into one corner of the den and started doing seated pushups, using the muscles in his arms and shoulders to lift his torso six inches up off of the wheelchair's seat, then slowly lowering himself. Up and down. Up and down . . . working the muscles in his body that still functioned.

Kelly turned back to the boys, curious. "Why did you choose this cabin to break into?"

"We didn't *really* break in," Jeremy objected in a high-pitched titter. "See, a back window was cracked open. We noticed it as we passed by, opened it just a little wider, and climbed through."

Chris turned a disapproving eye on Nathan. "I opened it this morning. The room stunk. He was smoking something gross in there last night."

Nathan looked hurt. "Just my regular cigarettes."

"It doesn't matter how we got in," Troy said. "We shouldn't have done it. But Jer, here, he was in a fix. Those goggles cost his parents a mint, and if he goes home without them they'll kill him."

"They will," Jeremy mumbled disconsolately.

"Whoever took them couldn't use them anyway," Kelly pointed out, "because of the special lenses."

Annette paced the floor, rubbing her forehead. "All right. I guess this makes sense. Did you boys find the goggles?"

"No," Jeremy said.

Nathan pushed to the front of the group. "How do we know they didn't snatch something of *ours?*" he complained. "You can't just let them go."

"Why don't we all go and look through our rooms to make sure nothing's missing—like money or anything else of value," Kelly suggested.

"Good idea," Jeff said. "Come on, guys."

He led Nathan, Chris, and Will into the bedroom the boys shared. The girls hurried toward theirs.

When Kelly, Angel, and Isabel returned to the den, Troy and Jeremy were still pressed against the wall where they'd left them. The two boys glanced nervously at each other, then at Annette, as if still worried she'd call the police.

A few minutes later, Jeff and the other Thomaston boys reappeared. "Everything seems to be accounted for," Jeff announced.

"Can we go now?" Jeremy whined, shifting from foot to foot like a little kid who needs to go to the bathroom.

"You can leave, but I want to know where you boys are staying in case anything turns up missing later," Annette said firmly.

"We're right around the bend, the A-frame three

cabins down the path," Troy said. "Mr. Parker is our chaperon."

Annette nodded and walked them to the door, still talking. "Let security take care of the search for the missing goggles," she advised as she followed them outside.

Kelly looked at Jeff. "Do you believe that?"

"You mean their excuse about the goggles?" he mumbled, crossing the room to look out the window. "I don't know. There's something weird about those two."

"I think the tall one is really cute," Angel said, twirling a strand of blonde hair around her finger.

Nathan rolled his eyes. "You think anything in pants is cute."

She shrugged. "It helps if a guy doesn't smoke like a chimney and drink constantly."

Nathan winced.

"Don't fight, guys," Kelly pleaded. "Come on, who wants pizza?"

"Frank won't eat pizza. He considers it junk food," Annette said. "Why don't you guys all go along. I'll stay here with him."

The next morning, Jeff stood at the top of the #4 chairlift and looked out over the snow-covered valley far below. He could see the modern wood-and-glass shapes of the hotel, with its restaurants and lounges, the lodge, and the parking lot. Off to the right was the nest of pine trees that hid their cabin and several dozen others. At the very bottom of the slope, snow-covered Deep Creek Lake stretched out like a lazy white cat in the sunshine.

"Did you change your mind?" a voice asked from behind Jeff.

He swung around to face Kelly. "About skiing the Chute?"

It was a black-diamond slope, one of the most difficult at Wisp. As an intermediate skier, he was supposed to stick to the trails marked with green circles or blue squares, the first being the very easiest for beginners, the second were meant for intermediate skiers.

"I wasn't thinking about that," he admitted.

"What were you thinking?" Kelly asked, stepping up closer and kissing him softly on the cheek.

"I was thinking I shouldn't have pushed you into going on this trip."

"I made up my own mind about coming."

"Yeah, after I mouthed off for weeks. I thought it would do you good to come back here. You know, give you a chance to say a final farewell to Brian."

Kelly blinked, her eyes stinging. "I really thought it would be okay. It's just hard, being here and trying to have fun . . . knowing Bri will never again get to do any of the things we're doing."

Jeff put his arm around her. "Why don't you ski a really super run for him?" he suggested.

Kelly liked the idea. "Sort of like a tribute?"

"Yeah."

She looked down the mountainside. To her far right was a fairly easy trail, Rabbit Run. Falling off to her left was the Chute, but that only stayed difficult for the first half of the descent. Dead center was a trail she hadn't tried yet, the Eye-Opener. It pitched downward at a dangerously steep angle and had been marked with double black diamonds to discourage anyone who wasn't an expert skier.

"All right," she said. "This one is for Brian."

Snapping her goggles into place over her eyes, she slipped the loops of her poles over her wrists.

"Wait! You're taking the Eye-Opener?" Jeff called.

"You got it." She pointed the tip of one pole

across the top of the mountain. "You take Rabbit Run, and I'll meet you back up here in half an hour."

Jeff laughed. "If you make it. That trail looks awful steep from here."

But what was the point of dedicating an easy run to Brian? There had to be a true challenge, a little danger. She thought how much Brian would have loved racing her down the mountainside.

Kelly shoved off with her poles. As soon as she was clear of the sheltering trees at the top, the wind whipped into her face, stealing her breath away. Icy crystals bit into her cheeks and flew up her nose. Branches of pine, hemlock, and spruce rushed past her in an evergreen blur.

Remembering one of Brian's first skiing tips to her, she fought the natural impulse to lean back against the steep grade to keep from going too fast. Instead, Kelly leaned forward and down the mountain.

As soon as her weight shifted over the toes of her boots, her skis stopped chattering against the icy ground and bit into the slick slope.

The trail was so steep she couldn't take it straight down. She brought the tips of her skis together then pressed hard on her right ski, making a wedge turn to the left. She cut across the snow-covered hill, slowing her descent. Slaloming back and forth across the trail between the double wall of trees, Kelly finally felt in control again. But she was aware of how light her body felt and how slack her muscles had become after a year of inactivity. She'd stopped weighing herself after she'd dropped twenty pounds. It had started to scare her.

Kelly looked around, still taking the trail cautiously, but now less involved with survival. The Eye-Opener was narrower than the beginner and intermediate trails. Through the trees, she glimpsed three skiers she didn't recognize moving slowly down a neighboring trail.

She wondered how Jeff was doing. He was becoming a good skier, but his technique wasn't controlled enough for a black diamond yet. Annette was very firm about which trails they were each allowed to take. Kelly wondered if she'd get in trouble for not clearing the Eye-Opener with her first.

A flash of red caught her eye between the trees. The person wearing the poppy-colored jacket looked like a girl. She was skiing cautiously down the beginner slope, just ahead of Kelly, screened by the trees that divided the two trails.

As Kelly flew past, the skier's head turned and she looked straight at Kelly, then quickly away.

Kelly's heart leapt into her throat. That face! It was familiar. Or was it just someone who looked like a person she knew, or had known?

Kelly gasped for breath, twisting around to look over her shoulder. The distraction was too much. For an instant, she forgot about the dangerously rough terrain. Suddenly she was slicing across an icy patch of ground, rocks and dead grass only sparsely covered with snow. She tried to turn, but couldn't get any traction on the treacherous surface. She brought the tips of her skis together and attempted to snowplow herself to a stop. Her heart raced as the ground scraped and bumped under her.

For seconds that felt like hours, Kelly fought the inevitable spill. But the speed at which she was traveling gave her no chance of regaining her balance.

She heard herself scream just before she completely lost control.

3

The only way Kelly could avoid the oncoming wall of trees was by pitching headlong into a snowbank.

She hit with an explosive thud and lay on the ground, breathing hard, observing the feathery green pine needles on the swaying branches overhead. After silently counting the bones that didn't seem to be broken and the joints that still seemed to function, she decided she'd probably be sore later that day but hadn't suffered anything worse than a muscle strain.

Carefully, Kelly sat up in the snow and checked out her surroundings while she caught her breath. The girl in the red jacket was nowhere around, but two figures were moving down the nearby beginner slope toward her.

At first, she thought the one in the black jacket might be Jeff. She struggled to her feet. She didn't want him to see that she'd wiped out; he'd tease her no end. *Expert skier, my eye,* he'd say.

But it wasn't Jeff. Troy skied toward her through the trees, followed by his friend Jeremy.

"Hey, are you all right?" Troy shouted, waving a mittened hand.

"Just great," she muttered, dusting herself off. Her poles were still looped around her wrists, but she'd have to look around for her skis. The bindings had released on impact, just as they were supposed to. One ski lay twenty feet down the middle of the slope, the other seemed to have disappeared completely.

"Wow," Jeremy said, wiping the fog from his glasses when he finally joined them, "this is a killer slope. What are *you* doing on it?"

Kelly glared at him. "I happen to be a very good skier."

"Could have fooled me," Troy laughed.

I hate boys, she thought. Kelly gave him a drop-dead look.

"Well," he added more diplomatically, "that *was* quite a dramatic crash landing."

"It wouldn't have happened if it hadn't been for that girl."

"What girl?" Jeremy asked.

Kelly flipped up her goggles and squinted back up the trail Troy and Jeremy had just come down. "A girl in a red jacket. You didn't see her?"

"What did she do?"

"Nothing, I just saw her face. She surprised me, and I lost my concentration." Kelly shook her head. "Never mind, you wouldn't understand."

"I'm getting cold," Jeremy complained. "If you're all right, maybe we should head on down and get some hot chocolate at the lodge. Right, Troy?" He looked hopefully at his friend.

Kelly hid a smile. Jeremy obviously wasn't enjoying himself. She wondered why he'd bothered to come to Wisp; he wasn't a skier. He didn't seem to like being outdoors any more than Nathan did.

"Why don't you ski the rest of the way down the beginner slope with us," Troy suggested.

Kelly shook her head. "No, I promised someone special I'd make it all the way down Eye-Opener. I'm going to do it." *For Brian,* she added silently.

"Being stubborn can be dangerous," Troy commented.

For a second his eyes lost their humor and turned

cold. Suddenly, he appeared much older than she. Kelly wondered what kind of life he'd led to give him that hard edge. A stray thought flashed through Kelly's head: *He knows about danger. He's seen it before.*

But then he grinned at her, and he again looked like a seventeen-year-old guy without a care in the world.

"If you're determined to finish this trail, I'll go with you," Troy said.

"What about me?" Jeremy whimpered. "I can't go on one of these black-diamond things! *I'd kill myself!*"

"He's right," Kelly said. "It really would be reckless for a beginner, or even an average skier." She was talking about Troy as much as she was about Jeremy. They both wore rental skis, and that was usually a sign the wearer hadn't skied much.

Troy pulled his goggles from around his neck, up and over his eyes. "Jeremy, you go on down Rabbit Run without me. I'll meet up with you later, down at the snack bar."

"But Troy, I don't think you should—"

"I'll be fine. You go ahead, just take it slow and you'll do okay."

"Wh-what if I fall and can't get up?" Jeremy stammered. His glasses were fogging up again.

"If you get into trouble, just wave down the ski patrol. They'll give you a ride to the bottom."

Looking disappointed but too tired to argue, Jeremy turned back into the trees and headed for Rabbit Run.

Kelly searched the gentle slope, looking again for the poppy-red jacket. She couldn't shake the eerie feeling that the girl, if it had been a girl, was someone she knew—someone who'd intentionally turned away because she didn't want her to know she was here.

"What was it about that girl that shook you so much?" Troy asked when Jeremy had moved away from them.

Kelly tromped down the hillside to retrieve her ski. "She just reminded me of someone I used to know."

"Who?"

"You sure ask a lot of questions."

"I'm just curious."

"I don't know why you should be." She didn't particularly want to make friends with a guy who broke into people's cabins. "You don't even know me, and we go to different schools."

"I'm interested in people," he said, as if that explained everything. "Look over there, isn't that your other ski sticking out of those bushes?"

"Yeah."

"I'll get it for you," Troy offered.

She watched him glide across the hill and into the trees, using his skis like skates to propel himself across the flat of the hill. Unlike most beginners, his balance looked rock solid. He seemed to know what he was doing.

Troy brought back her ski. She lined both of them up across the hill, and stepped into the bindings, then jammed her heels down to lock her boots into the metal jaws attached to the skis.

"Are you sure you want to do this?" Kelly asked. "I can take it pretty slow, but if the slope gets away from you, you might end up in the trees like I did . . . or worse."

"Just watch out for yourself," Troy said, smiling confidently.

It didn't take her long to discover why he'd seemed so amused with her concern. Troy York was an excellent skier. He worked the mountain to his advantage, cutting across its face with strong, controlled curving actions. By slaloming wide, side to

22

side across the trail, he was able to move gradually down even the steepest slopes.

At first, Kelly let him set the pace, but as the rough terrain and icy patches gave way to new machine-made snow, she let herself go. Zooming past Troy, she sent icy granules flying from her ski blades as she slalomed right, left, right again, narrowing her path and letting gravity carry her along, faster and faster.

She laughed out loud, sure she'd left a startled Troy far behind. But a moment later, as the freezing air whooshed past her, she caught sight of his black-and-purple jacket moving in on her right side.

"How'd you catch up?" she shouted, going faster still.

"No sweat!" he yelled back as he passed her. But she could tell he was breathing hard with the exertion, and she laughed again, feeling excited.

It was almost like skiing with Brian again. He'd been as close to a brother as she'd ever had, and just as good a skier as she was. Being with Brian had been fun. Being with Troy felt good.

"Race you to the bottom!" she shouted.

"Winner buys sodas!"

And they were off.

Kelly carved narrower cuts across the hill. But she didn't take chances on another fall. She avoided icy spots and stuck to the deep, new snow.

Troy plunged ahead of her, then seemed to ease up.

"If you let me win, I'll never speak to you again!" Kelly shouted.

She saw him grin before he pointed his skis straight down the hill. Bending in a racer's crouch to get less air resistance, Troy streaked down the mountain—purple lightning against white snow. The sight of him took her breath away.

Kelly joined him at the bottom a few seconds

after he'd swerved to a sudden stop at the bottom of the chairlift, spraying snow on a bunch of squealing little kids in the Play-Ski class.

"How did you learn to ski like that?" she gasped, whipping off her goggles.

He hesitated for a fraction of a second. "My dad taught me." Troy yanked off his earwarmers. Sweat streamed from the dark fringes of his hair. His eyes danced with excitement. "Man, that was the best run I've had in I don't know how long."

"It was fun," she agreed. "Next time I'll beat you."

"Not if I don't want you to."

Kelly giggled. "We'll see about that. Come on. I guess I owe you a soda."

After they exchanged their ski boots for hiking boots and stored their gear, Kelly ordered a diet root beer and Troy had a lemon-lime soda. They sat in the snack bar and shared a bag of barbecue-flavored potato chips. Kelly ate one chip then took a second, remembering she hadn't had any break-fast that day. She wasn't really sure when she'd last eaten. She just wasn't hungry.

"So, about this girl in the red jacket," Troy said, as if their conversation had never been interrupted, "what was she doing that caught your attention?"

"I told you, she wasn't *doing* anything. I just felt as if I recognized her, but it couldn't have been who I thought it was."

"Who did you think it was?"

Kelly groaned. "You're a pest."

Troy shrugged and munched on his chips.

She sighed sadly. "I thought it was a girl I once knew, Paula Schultz."

"She was your friend?"

"I *hated* her!" Kelly ground out, surprised that the words came out so full of bitterness. "She killed my best friend."

24

Troy set down his soda can and studied her face. "*Killed* as in *murdered?*"

"Yes . . . no, not really. It was more of an accident, I guess." Then she told Troy the short version of her last trip to Deep Creek Lake. "According to Paula, she panicked when Brian took her suicide talk seriously. They were out in a rowboat on the lake, and he fell in. She told the police she tried to save him, but the water was too cold, and it was dark . . ."

Kelly's voice drifted off. She shook her head helplessly before continuing. "I guess she didn't want anyone to find out that she'd been the reason Brian died. When Nathan, one of the boys in our ski club, discovered the truth, she tried to kill him. Then I found out and she came after me. Paula totally went off the deep end."

Troy blew out a long breath. "Sounds like she must have been a little light in her loafers from the beginning. I'll bet they've got her locked away somewhere. Hope they threw away the key."

"Last I heard, she was in a special hospital for people who are emotionally disturbed."

"Then it couldn't have been her that you saw," Troy stated, gazing through the wide glass windows of the snack bar that overlooked the lake.

"I guess not." Kelly finished her soda and scrunched up the empty chip bag. Her chest felt hot and tight. Talking about Brian and Paula made her feel as if she couldn't breathe. "I'm going for a walk. I have to get some air," she blurted out as she pushed up from the table and ran for the door.

Kelly wasn't surprised to find Troy beside her by the time she'd crossed the street and started down the wooded slope toward the lake. But she wished he'd go away so that she could think.

That girl had looked so much like Paula; seeing

her had shaken Kelly even worse than she'd at first realized.

For the few minutes she'd been racing Troy, she'd felt healthy and strong . . . completely escaped from the past. Maybe it had been a surge of adrenaline that had carried her along. Skiing was suddenly an effortless act, like riding a huge ocean breaker to shore. Now, she felt weak and light-headed.

You should eat something, she told herself, repeating her father's frequent words. He worried about her. She'd lost so much weight since Brian died.

I'll eat tonight, she thought.

They walked down through the trees to the shore of the lake. There was a path around it, but it was hidden by snow. In another month, there would be soft brown earth and daffodils. Now, everything looked as cold as death. She wished Brian could have been here instead of Troy.

But Troy, for all his nosiness, wasn't trying to annoy her, she realized. He was being quiet now, as if he understood she had to sort through her feelings. That's nice of him, she thought.

They walked in silence nearly a mile around the north end of the lake. Then she felt Troy tense up beside her and jerk to a halt.

Kelly looked up from the path. Troy was staring across the lake, and she followed the direction of his puzzled eyes.

Walking across the ice was a girl in a bright red ski jacket.

Kelly reached out and grabbed Troy's arm. "That's her! The girl I saw."

"We're too far away to make out her face," he said.

Kelly drew her tongue across wind-chapped lips. "What's that she's carrying?"

From a distance, all she could see was a colorful blur in the girl's hands. She was stepping gingerly over the snow-covered ice, as if afraid it might crack and she'd fall through. But with a winter as severe as they'd had, and no spring thaw in sight, Kelly was sure the ice would hold.

The girl turned, stopped and looked around her as if she'd lost something. At last, Kelly could make out the shape in her hands. It was a brightly colored wreath.

"Looks like she's leaving flowers on the ice," Troy whispered.

A brittle chill nipped at Kelly's bones. "A memorial wreath," she choked out. "She's leaving a memorial for someone who drowned."

4

Troy touched Kelly on the arm as tears washed down her cheeks. "The flowers might not be for your friend. A lake like this with so many tourists around every summer . . . there are always accidents."

Kelly nodded, unable to speak.

But she couldn't convince herself. That girl . . . *that girl* had stared at her as if she had recognized her, too. And now she was laying flowers over the water where Brian had drowned.

"Come on," Kelly said, "I've got to get a closer look at her."

She ran blindly toward the edge of the lake, her heart in her throat. Her brain told her she had to be wrong. Paula—who'd once tried to kill her, who was responsible for the death of her best friend—had been put away in a place where she couldn't hurt anyone else.

The police had told her father just that. "Don't worry, Mr. Peterson. Your daughter is perfectly safe now. The Schultz girl is locked up good and tight."

But another part of her, deep down inside her body, clicked off warnings as she dodged between rough tree trunks, momentarily losing sight of the lake. *Be careful! Turn back! It's her, it's her . . . it's her!*

She couldn't turn back. A hunger that never

showed up at mealtimes seized her now. She was incapable of ignoring it.

Trudging through the crusty snow at the lake's frozen lip, Kelly peered across the ice. The girl in the red jacket was no longer there.

Kelly drew in a slow breath, trying to steady nerves that were pinging inside of her like popping corn. Had she imagined that girl?

No. Troy had seen her too. He'd said so.

Slowly she turned, expecting he'd be right behind her. Instead, she found herself face to face with a painfully familiar face.

"Paula!" Kelly gasped.

"Hello, Kel. How have you been?" The girl's skin was so pale it gave the illusion that light off the snow was showing right through it. The wisps of soft blonde hair framing her face seemed cotton-candy fragile. A pinch between fingers would dissolve them.

"Hello, Paula," Kelly whispered. She couldn't think of anything more to say. But with every second hatred boiled closer to the surface.

Troy jogged lightly to Kelly's side and stood there, looking at the other girl with interest. "I went back to lock up the skis. Thought it might be a good idea since we weren't going to pick them up right away."

Kelly nodded. She couldn't take her eyes off of Paula. *Why didn't you die with him?* she thought. *Or instead of him.* Brian had been such a good guy. It wasn't fair.

"I guess you're wondering why I'm here," Paula said at last. Her voice seemed no more than a shadowy reminder of her real self. Kelly remembered that when she'd wanted her way with Brian, she'd sounded tough enough.

"Yeah, sort of," Kelly admitted stiffly.

"I had to come back here." Paula's eyes met Kelly's for an instant, then dodged away. "The doctors at the hospital, they kept trying to make me remember everything . . . how it was with Brian in the boat. How it had tipped and I'd tried, *really tried* to help him, but I couldn't."

Kelly blinked, unable to speak over the lump in her throat.

"I did, honest, you have to believe me," Paula continued. "I jumped into the water, but it was so cold . . . so very cold that November night. And it was darker than any night I can remember. I reached down into the water, and for a moment I thought I had hold of Brian's jacket, and I tried to pull him up. But he slipped out of my fingers, and then I couldn't see or hear anything. He was gone."

Kelly felt Troy put a hand on her shoulder and realized she was sobbing softly. She sniffled back hot tears. "You should have told someone what happened!" she cried out. "We might have been able to do something."

"It was too late," Paula whispered. "Oh Kelly, I was so afraid of what everyone would think. I didn't mean anything bad to happen to Brian. I just thought I could make him stay with me, not go away to school. I never really wanted us to kill ourselves."

"But . . . but even after it happened. If you'd explained it all, we would have understood. The police would have had to believe you."

Paula lifted one shoulder in a wobbly shrug. "Maybe. I was terrified. I wasn't thinking straight. And I couldn't stand the thought of people saying I'd killed Brian, so I pretended a stranger had attacked us."

Kelly bit down on her bottom lip and glared at Paula. "That's not all you did."

Paula winced. "I know. I didn't understand for a

long time what I'd done to you and to Nathan—how I'd nearly killed both of you. I must have been so crazy with grief over Brian . . ." She broke off and stared down at the frozen ground, her head shaking from side to side as if it were on a spring, as if it were one of those kewpie dolls people used to put in the back windows of their cars. "I'm so sorry. It took the doctors a long time to help me remember what I'd done, and then I didn't want to believe it . . . it was so horrible."

Kelly looked skeptically at Paula. Was she telling the truth?

Troy stepped forward. "Horrible or not, you were at least partly responsible for one boy's death, and you tried to kill two other kids. I can't believe a psychiatric hospital let you walk out just a year later."

Paula squinted at him, as if trying to place him. "Do I know you?"

"This is Troy York. His ski club is here for the week, like ours."

"None of this is your business," Paula snapped. "This is between Kelly and me."

"Paula!" Kelly gasped. "That's rude."

Troy shook his head. "It just doesn't make sense she'd be allowed to leave the hospital until the doctors thought—"

"I'm cured," Paula broke in. "They told me I could go home."

"Really?" Kelly said.

"Yes." Paula looked away from her. "But they said there was one more thing I had to do. My counselor told me to come to the lake and tell Brian how sorry I was . . ." Tears filled Paula's eyes.

Kelly saw in Paula's pale face the signs of pain so like her own. Paula had loved Brian, maybe not in a healthy way, not like *she* had cared for him.

Kelly glanced at Troy, who was frowning doubtfully at Paula. But she couldn't stay angry with her any longer.

"I believe you," Kelly said impulsively. "I believe you're sorry about what happened."

With the words came a sudden sensation of her body settling into a peacefulness she hadn't known since before the accident. The hate seemed to pass through her and into the chill air.

Kelly took a deep breath and wiped her own tears away. "Why don't you come back with us to the cabin, Paula. The ski club rented a place up the hill from here. You can stay for supper, or longer if you like. A lot of the kids you know are there."

Paula shot a worried look at Troy. "I'm afraid of what they'll think of me."

"If I tell them I've asked you to come, they'll have to understand," Kelly reassured her. "It'll be okay."

Kelly and Troy carried their skis on their shoulders. Paula followed close behind. It took fifteen minutes to make the trek up the mountain through the woods to the cabins.

Jeff was waiting for them on the porch.

"Hey!" Kelly cried, glad to see him.

He smiled at her, then frowned and stuck his hands in his pockets when he spotted Troy. "Where have you been? I waited at the summit for ages, but you never showed."

Kelly belatedly remembered their plans to meet. "Oh, I'm sorry. I'll bet you got really cold standing up there, waiting for me."

"I gave up after an hour and came back here to warm up," he grumbled. Then his eyes shifted again, taking in Paula. Jeff's jaw dropped two inches.

Kelly stepped forward. "Paula came to leave a

wreath for Brian on the lake. The doctors say she's okay now."

Jeff closed his mouth and said nothing, but he didn't look any more convinced than Troy had a few minutes earlier.

"Come on inside," Kelly said, gently taking Paula's arm. "You can make up your mind about staying after you've met everyone." She turned to Troy. "Want to come in for a soda?"

Troy hesitated, observing Jeff, who'd wrapped a possessive arm around Kelly as they moved toward the cabin door. "Maybe I should go along. My friends will be looking for me."

Kelly smiled at him. "Maybe we'll see you tonight on the trails. We ski under the lights every night."

Troy nodded. "Yeah. Maybe."

Kelly watched him stride away, across the snow and into the trees, then she turned to follow Paula into the cabin.

"So what's with him?" Jeff asked, holding her back.

"What do you mean?"

"I mean, you stood me up to ski with *him.*"

Kelly stared at Jeff, astonished. They'd been going together for over a year, and he'd never once acted jealous. "You make it sound as if I had a date with him or something!"

"Well, it sure sounds like you did," Jeff said.

Kelly huffed and tried to step around him to go inside the cabin. Jeff blocked her way. She glared at him furiously.

Little by little, he seemed to let go of his fury.

"I'm sorry, Kel. I didn't mean to yell at you. I was just ticked off, seeing that guy with you after we'd made plans and . . ." He shrugged.

Kelly reached out and hugged Jeff, hard. "I *really*

am sorry. I just forgot about our plans, and I didn't think there was anything wrong with skiing the rest of the way down with Troy and having a soda with him."

"There isn't, I guess," Jeff admitted. "Come on. Nathan's in the den. We've probably missed the best part. By now he's seen Paula and wet his pants."

Kelly laughed out loud. "I wouldn't blame him—poor guy."

Paula's reunion with the other students didn't go as badly as Jeff had anticipated. Although Nathan made a point of sitting on the opposite side of the room from Paula, he was subdued and polite to her. At least as polite as Nathan was capable of being.

Kelly headed for the kitchen to make coffee and hot chocolate for everyone, since no one wanted sodas. As she passed Nathan, she glanced curiously at him. His eyes were red and glassy. She wondered if he'd smuggled booze in his luggage like he'd done the last time they'd come to Deep Creek. She didn't smell anything on his breath; but that might not mean anything. He could have been drinking vodka.

As more of the kids returned to the cabin, Annette and Frank started to prepare for supper. Paula offered to help since she'd been invited to stay.

Will followed her into the kitchen, flirting casually with her the way he did with every girl he met. He'd once suggested to Kelly that she drop Jeff for him, but she knew how long his interest in one girl lasted. A weekend was a long-term commitment for Will. Besides, she had no intention of cheating on Jeff, or dumping him.

As she glanced out into the kitchen, she saw Paula laughing, her eyes blue and alive again.

Jeff leaned toward Kelly on the couch. "Does

Will know her history? Better warn him not to go on any boat rides with her."

Kelly elbowed him in the ribs. "That's not funny!"

"I'm serious. Some shrink may believe she's cured, but I still think she's spooky. I wouldn't go out with her."

"Of course you wouldn't," Kelly teased. "You've got me."

"That's not what I meant."

She sighed. "I know what you mean." Then something struck her. "Maybe Paula's the one we should warn."

"Why?"

"Will's such a fast talker. Every party we've been to, he picks up a different girl."

Jeff laughed. "Just because he's popular—"

"It's more than that. I don't think someone as . . . as"—she searched for the right word—"as vulnerable as Paula should date someone like Will."

"So warn her," Jeff said. "Maybe she'll listen."

After a supper of spaghetti, garlic bread, salad, and strawberry gelatin topped with Fun Whip, half the group changed back into ski clothes. As Jeff pulled on thermal underwear then stepped into his ski pants, he thought about his fight with Kelly. He felt awful about it.

He'd acted like a jerk, accused her of flirting with that guy Troy while she was going steady with him. She wasn't that kind of girl. If she wanted to date someone else, she'd say so. She'd come out and tell him she wanted to break up . . . wouldn't she?

Sometimes he thought about that.

Most of the time, though, he worried more about Kelly's health. She'd never seemed to get over Brian's death. She lost a lot of weight and ate only

35

when he took her out to a restaurant and ordered things for her. Even then, she picked at her food.

That night, Jeff skied with Kelly down one of the two intermediate slopes that had been illuminated for night skiing. They didn't talk much, just concentrated on moving down the mountain. It gave him a lot of time to think.

Jeff liked being with Kelly. She was smart and pretty, and she was nice to everyone. If they broke up, he'd miss her a lot. But he hadn't really thought about her being with another guy, until he'd seen her walking up the hill through the woods with Troy.

His gut burned, and a molten rage welled up inside of him. Jeff cut straight over a mogul, was airborne for three seconds, then landed on the crusty snow with a *whack.*

"Hey, Hot Dog, that was good!" Kelly called out, laughing.

"You ain't seen nothing yet." He wanted to impress her. He crested another mogul, then another. It wasn't until the fourth that he leaned too far to one side and crashed in a cloud of snow between two of the humps.

Kelly side-stepped up the hill to him. "You all right?"

"Fine," he grumbled, retrieving his skis.

"That was pretty daring stuff for you," she commented.

"You make it sound like I'm a novice or something."

"No. But you're usually cautious. That's smart skiing, knowing your limitations."

He knew she was just being logical, but it still irritated him. *I'll bet old Troy isn't cautious. You seem pretty impressed with him!* he thought glumly.

"Listen, Kelly, I know you want to ski faster,"

Jeff said. "Why don't you go on ahead." He looked back up the hill. "Chris and Isabel are on their way down. I'll join them."

"Are you sure?" Kelly asked, sounding disappointed. "I don't mind slowing down. Everything's so pretty and romantic in the moonlight."

She lifted her face and closed her eyes, waiting for him to kiss her. But he didn't feel like kissing Kelly just then, not while he was still brooding about Troy. "Go on," he said. "We'll make the next run together."

Kelly reluctantly skied away from him, cutting graceful curves in the snow, down the mountainside. She moved almost effortlessly on skis, as if the rhythm came naturally to her.

Somehow, all of his years of running track didn't translate to skiing. He felt stiff and mechanical on skis. He had to think about every move.

With a sigh, Jeff turned and looked back up the slope. Chris and Isabel were getting closer. Chris's big body and wide, dark face stood out against the snow. Isabel's honey-brown skin made her look as if she had a great tan. Most kids didn't realize she was a quarter Navaho Indian, a background she was proud of. Her long black hair streamed out behind her like a comet's dark tail.

They were moving slowly, then stopped. Jeff waited impatiently, wanting to get started on the way down. But Chris was shouting something at Isabel, and she turned away from him and pushed off down the hill again, a pinched expression on her lips. He wondered what they'd been arguing about.

When they stopped a second time, he looked around for someone else to ski with. Nathan had stayed behind at the cabin—probably to drink. Since he'd broken up with Angel he never did much else. He was surprised Nathan had bothered signing up for the trip at all—but then he didn't have much of a home life. He probably figured anything was better than spending spring break at home.

On the other side of the trees Jeff could see Paula and Will, riding on a snowmobile. The vehicle stopped, and Will turned on the seat. Paula draped her arms around his neck and kissed him.

Jeff chuckled to himself, thinking how irritated Kelly was going to be when he told her what he'd seen. Things seemed out of her hands.

He still thought Will had more to worry about than Paula. After all, *she* was the certified psycho! Or she had been . . .

Since it didn't look as if he was going to have any company on his way down, Jeff started off on his own.

He'd only gone a few hundred feet when someone whisked past him. It was Chris. A minute later, Isabel came along, skiing much more slowly. Her eyes were red and puffy, as if she'd been crying.

"Hey, you all right?" Jeff asked, gliding over beside her.

She wiped at her eyes with the back of one mitten. "Yeah. I guess."

"What's wrong?"

"Oh, it's Chris. He thinks I'm being nosy. He says I should mind my own business."

Isabel started down the hill again, but Jeff stopped her, not sure she could see where she was going. "Why would he say something like that?"

"Because of Kelly." She looked at him apologetically. "I'm really worried about her, Jeff. Three weeks ago, we had a health screening in gym class. Kelly didn't want to get weighed. Mrs. Cummings made her get on the scale after everyone else had left . . . but I saw it."

"So?"

"She weighed 90 pounds."

Jeff shook his head. "You must be wrong. That's awful low."

"Of course it is. Kelly's five-seven, a lot taller than I am. We both have a medium bone structure. She should weigh more than that. Last year, she weighed 118—I know because we were guessing each other's weights one night over at my house."

Somehow Jeff knew she was right. He just hadn't realized Kelly had dropped that low.

"I'm really afraid for her," Isabel said. "She should go to a doctor, but she won't listen to me."

"Is there anything I can do?" Jeff asked.

"Talk to her. She and I are best friends, and that counts for a lot. But you're her boyfriend, and she really respects you."

"Maybe we should talk to her together, you and me at the same time."

Isabel shook her head. "She might feel as if we're ganging up on her."

"Okay," he agreed. "I'll try."

5

Kelly waited patiently for Jeff at the bottom of the hill. She was a faster skier, but he was getting better every day. She figured he shouldn't be far behind her. She watched the shadowy figures glide down the snowy hillside. Although high-intensity lamps lined the slopes, they couldn't cut through the dark like real sunlight. From this distance, she couldn't make out faces.

She was sitting on a bench near the end of the lift line, still waiting for Jeff, when Angel sauntered over to her. "Hi. Aren't you going up again?"

"I'll probably take two more runs and call it quits for the night," Kelly said.

"Waiting for Jeff?"

"Yeah."

"He'll be here soon," Angel commented. "He stopped to talk to Isabel. I saw them on my way down."

Kelly's eye was drawn by a sudden motion. She turned to see Will Grant zoom across the snow in front of them with Paula clinging to the back of his snowmobile, giggling with delight.

"She sure works fast," Angel said.

"Or *he* does." Well, at least Paula looked happy. Kelly had never thought she'd want to see Brian's girlfriend enjoying life again, but things seemed different now.

40

"By the way, have you seen Troy around tonight?" Angel asked.

"I don't know if he planned on coming," Kelly said. "His friend Jeremy seems sort of jittery on skis. I'll bet he wouldn't want to ski at night."

Angel sighed. "Too bad. Troy is really cool."

"You think so?"

"Sure. He seems different from most of the boys at school. More mature . . . I don't know, different somehow."

"I was thinking that too," Kelly admitted.

"Anyway, if you see him, tell him I'd like to—"

Kelly squinted into the shadows behind the lodge. "Isn't that Troy over there?"

Angel turned and followed her glance. She smiled triumphantly. "Oh cool, he's not with that dork Jeremy. I think I'll go ask him if he wants to ski with me."

Troy had been watching the kids from Thomaston High for two days. At first he'd hung around outside their cabin, focusing his attention on Nathan. He seemed the most obvious target—always sneaking drinks behind the chaperons' backs, acting like he hated everyone, even himself. A classic loser.

But it didn't take him long to decide the kid was small pickings. Troy turned his attention to the others.

Sometimes he skied down the slopes with a few of the students, joining in their conversations, pretending he was having as much fun as they were. Other times, he watched them from the trees, unseen, waiting for the right moment.

He'd shadowed Kelly and her boyfriend to the midpoint of one slope, then hid behind a large tree to observe them and catch what he could of their conversation. When Kelly had gone on alone, he'd stayed behind and watched Jeff. At first Troy wondered if Jeff was cheating on Kelly with the pretty Native American girl, but the two had only talked then hugged in a brother/sister kind of way and skied on.

He'd left them, knowing he hadn't yet found what he was looking for. When he did find it, he'd close the trap quickly, not taking any chances.

Troy was watching Kelly and Angel behind the lodge when Kelly snapped around and spotted him, although he'd thought he was being careful. Before he could duck out of sight, Angel bounced across the packed snow to where he stood.

"Hi, Troy!" she called out cheerfully.

Troy felt anything but cheerful at the moment.

Angel was dressed in a fitted ski suit, pure white from throat to ankles. Her pale hair was swept back from her face with a wide, white angora headband. Angel's strange-colored eyes—somewhere between blue and lavender—gleamed at him from porcelain skin, gently flushed by the cold.

She was pretty, Troy thought, but a little unsettling too.

"Oh, hi," he returned.

"Want some company? I mean, if you're going up for another run." She pointed to the top of Wisp.

"I'm a little wiped," he said. "Thought I'd better stop before exhaustion sets in. Skiing tired can be dangerous."

Angel laughed. "You sound like my father . . . so serious. I know that's a good safety rule. But you can't get hurt if you're with me."

He frowned at her. "Huh?"

"Think of me as a good-luck charm." She grinned at him, as if savoring a secret.

"I still don't understand."

"Ever hear of angels?"

"Well, sure, like at Christmas time. 'Angels we have heard on high,' that sort of thing, like in Christmas carols."

"No. I mean *everyday* angels—the kind who keep watch over you and protect you from harm."

Troy stared at her. "Are you serious?"

Her eyes sparkled. "Of course I'm serious. Angels have to be, they're not allowed to lie."

Good grief, he thought, *just what I need. A Loony Tune in the flesh.*

"Just because your name, or your nickname, is Angel . . . that doesn't mean you really are one," he reasoned patiently.

"But I am," she insisted in a soft voice. "I'm here with my sisters to look after whoever needs help. And I have a very strong feeling that *you* need *a lot* of help, Troy York."

Troy stiffened and took a step backwards. This girl was giving him the definite willies. "I don't need anyone looking after me." Besides, he had work to do, and he couldn't very well do it with some ditzy girl trailing after him. "I still don't think I want to ski any more tonight." He started to back away from her. "Maybe some other time. Okay?"

Her pretty eyes gleamed a little less brightly. "Okay, I guess. You know where I'll be."

Paula watched Will ride away up the mountain after he'd dropped her off on the path. She felt so excited. He was such a hunk, and he seemed to like her too. She could think of nothing but him all the way back to the cabin.

When she got there, she expected to find someone inside since only half of the group had said they would be skiing. Anyway, it was after 10 p.m. and most of the kids would be stopping for the night.

But when Paula let herself in the front door, no

one was in the den or kitchen. The stale odor of burnt tobacco lingered in the air, making her feel like choking.

"Anyone home?" she called out, dropping the skis and boots she'd rented behind the door. She'd arranged to keep them for a few days so that she wouldn't have to keep turning them in at the end of every skiing session. "Hey, it's too early to be sleeping!"

She peeked into the bedrooms. All three were empty.

"Guess you guys changed your minds," she murmured. Still, it seemed odd that no one had stayed behind, not even Nathan, who did nothing but grouse about the cold, or Mr. Riley, who didn't like going outside because his wheelchair got stuck in the snow.

Paula picked up a magazine and flopped on the couch, but she felt restless. The cabin was too quiet, too empty.

Popping up from the couch, Paula ran to the nearest window. She lifted the calico curtain and peered out through the glass. The Rileys' Jeep was gone.

Well, that explained Mr. Riley's absence. Kelly had told her it was fitted with a special hand-operated brake and accelerator so that he could drive it.

But where could he have gone at this hour? Maybe Annette was with him and they'd gone off on their own for an hour of privacy. Paula yawned.

She was tired, very tired. She wasn't used to all this fresh air and exercise. It felt great, but she wasn't sure she could stay awake much longer.

At the institute, it was lights out at 9 p.m., every night. By now all of the girls in her ward would be asleep, or pretending to be.

Paula smiled. By now the nurses would have

realized she was missing. And they wouldn't have a clue where to start looking for her, she thought smugly.

Paula walked into the kitchen and helped herself to a can of cola from the fridge, making sure it was the kind with caffeine in it. She didn't want to fall asleep before the others returned and miss all the fun. It had been so long since she'd had such a good time. She couldn't remember the last time she'd laughed and shrieked with delight, the way she had while riding across the snowy hills with Will.

Thirstily, she gulped down half the can . . . then stopped, the cool aluminum cylinder poised in her fingers. She listened.

The sound came again. A soft scraping. It seemed to be coming from one of the back rooms.

Putting the can down on the table, Paula moved cautiously toward the girls' room and looked inside. No one was there. *Mice,* she thought with a shiver, *I'll bet an old cabin like this has loads of them.* But she decided she'd better check out the other rooms anyway, just in case it was anything more serious. She'd heard the kids talking about someone breaking in.

In the boys' room, she again found no one, but the window was open. An icy breeze slithered across the room like an invisible serpent. She shoved the window down, and turned to leave, and nearly tripped over a corner of a suitcase that was protruding from beneath one of the beds.

"Boys," she mumbled, "they're such slobs."

Thinking of Will and wondering if he was as disorganized as most guys she'd known, Paula kicked the case further under the bed to make sure no one hurt themselves tripping over it. Her toe struck something hard. It rattled inside the case.

"Gee," she whispered, "hope I didn't break anything."

Paula knelt on the floor and pulled the soft-sided suitcase out again, further than before, and lifted the lid. She peered at the tumble of jerseys, sweaters, and thermal underclothes. Nothing here looked as if it would rattle.

Reaching beneath the layers of clothing, she felt around. Her fingers brushed against something hard and cold, something metallic with a hand grip shaped like the six-shooter water pistol her little brother had played with the last summer she'd been home.

She carefully wrapped her fingers around the object and brought out her hand. An automatic pistol gleamed dully in the moonlight streaming through the window. From the weight and deadly feel of it, she was pretty sure it wasn't a toy.

Paula's breath caught in her throat. Who would bring *a gun* on a class trip? Who of the kids at her old school would even own a gun?

Her eyes shifted again to the window. Had someone sneaked in and planted the weapon? Was that what she'd heard a few minutes earlier? But why would anyone do that?

Paula sat down on the floor and pushed the weapon a safe distance away from her on the floor. She stared at it, thinking hard. Her head ached dully, and she suddenly felt confused.

What would Dr. Raymond, her counselor, tell her to do in a situation like this? *Take your problem to someone who has the experience to help you deal with it.*

Yes, she thought, *that's exactly what I'll do!* She closed the suitcase, slid it back under the bed, and picked up the gun.

"Where are you going with that?" a voice snapped.

Paula swung around, the pistol heavy in her hand. "Oh, it's you!" She smiled warily. "I heard a noise in here and . . . Look what I found!" She laughed uneasily, for the first time realizing she hadn't even looked to see whose suitcase the weapon had been in. "Can you imagine someone bringing a *gun* on a ski trip?"

The answering laugh was empty, cold, and sinister. "You shouldn't have been snooping around."

The back of Paula's neck tingled uncomfortably. "It's no big deal. If it's yours and you want it back, I'll give it to you." She held out her hand, the gun resting on her palm. "I just don't think you should be carrying something like this around. Here, take it."

"Thank you." But after accepting the pistol, its owner didn't move.

The tingle intensified to an irritating prickle as Paula realized her way to the door was blocked.

"If you're worried that I'll tell someone about your having that thing," Paula said, "I promise I won't."

"You probably mean that, Paula. You're a nice girl, but you've got a lousy history."

"You mean because of what happened up here before? When my boyfriend drowned?"

"No, because you talk to shrinks and tell them things that bother you. You might just blab the wrong thing . . . then I'd be in a real fix. In fact, it looked like you were on your way to show someone the gun."

"The police would just take the gun away from you." She suddenly felt bold. After all, *she* was in the right this time. "You shouldn't have one anyway."

"That's just the tip of the iceberg, Paula. Just the tip, and I can't let you or anyone else find the rest of it."

The barrel of the automatic rose slowly, then leveled on Paula's chest. For the longest seconds of her life, she looked down the dark barrel of that gun. She could hear nothing above the *bang-bang-bang* of her own pulse exploding in her ears.

Then the gun's owner seemed to have second thoughts. "I can't shoot you. That would make things worse."

Paula let out a weak sigh of relief.

A stubby kitchen knife appeared from inside the jacket.

Paula stepped backward and shrieked, "You can't just kill a person for—"

The fist holding the knife shot forward. Paula didn't have a chance to move aside. A searing pain rushed through her body. As her knees buckled, a soft whimper escaped her lips. The room spun, flew out of focus, then turned as black as if someone had pulled down a heavy shade, blocking the sun's light from the room . . . only it was nighttime, and the light was coming from the electric bulb overhead . . . Where had the light gone?

She felt herself hit the floor, then the heaviness of the pain left her body. Footsteps moved slowly away from her. She heard a door creak, then creak again . . . and there was silence.

It's like slipping beneath warm water, she thought. *Like submerging in a pool of your own existence.* She thought of Brian, one last time. For months after he'd died, she'd wanted to join him. Why did it have to happen now—just when life had started meaning something to her again?

With a reluctant shudder, Paula softly died.

Kelly and Jeff hiked up the path toward the cabin, skis and poles balanced on their shoulders. Jeff seemed especially quiet as they tramped over the packed snow.

"So, what did you and Isabel talk about?" Kelly asked at last.

Jeff looked startled. "Isabel?"

"Yeah, Angel told me she saw you two standing on the trail, talking."

"Oh."

"Were you helping her with her skiing technique?" Kelly asked. Isabel was just a beginner.

"Yeah," Jeff said, "that's it. She's having trouble with her wedge turns."

Kelly squinted suspiciously at Jeff. He looked so guilty. She'd never known him to lie. She wondered why he was doing it now.

"Listen, Kel, we have to talk about something," he said abruptly.

"Sure. What is it?"

"It's the way you've been eating . . . or *not* eating."

She turned away from him, feeling a wave of hot embarrassment. "What are you going to do? Lecture me like my father always does?"

"I'm just worried about you."

"Don't worry. I'm fine."

"Some days, I think you don't eat at all."

"That's not true!" she snapped. "I just choose carefully what I eat. And sometimes I'm not hungry."

He rolled his eyes. "You should see a doctor. You've lost too much weight. There are diseases called eating disorders that—"

"Have you and Isabel been plotting? Is that what this is all about?" she snapped, furious with both of them. What right did her friends have to butt into her private life?

"No, not really." He raked his fingers through his short hair and looked at her sadly. "Is this because of Brian?"

She glared at him. "It's because I want to eat when I feel like it. I don't have to do anything that makes me feel bad."

He seemed to think for a minute. "You're not afraid of getting fat, are you? I mean, for acting in the plays or because of me."

She hadn't worried about that in a long time, but it made no difference. She didn't want to talk about it, especially not with Jeff, because if he was talking about what she thought he was talking about—anorexia—she was totally grossed out, and she expected he was too. How could he love someone who intentionally starved herself?

That wasn't what she was doing. She just didn't have time, or the appetite to eat some days. Why was everyone getting so bent out of shape?

She opened her mouth to tell him to leave her alone when Nathan, Isabel, and Chris stepped onto the path from an adjoining trail.

Jeff looked at Nathan. "I thought you weren't going skiing tonight."

"I didn't," he grumbled. "Just wanted to get some air. Gets stuffy in that old shack."

"That's because you're puffing like a locomotive on those disgusting cigarettes," Kelly commented.

"Nag," Nathan sneered, and aimed an impolite gesture at her with one hand.

Jeff took a step forward and pulled back his right fist as if about to deposit it in Nathan's face. Kelly guessed he was more frustrated with *her* than with Nathan, who was only being his obnoxious self.

She hastily stepped between the two boys and put a hand on Jeff's arm. "Forget it. I shouldn't have said anything." But she didn't apologize to Nathan. He was so inconsiderate, filling the cabin with smoke and making the place miserable for the rest of the group.

They reached the cabin in time to see Will and Angel helping Frank Riley pull sacks of groceries out of the back of the Jeep. Although he was in a wheelchair, Frank was able to reach inside the vehicle, haul out two or three bags at a time, and hold them on his lap while he rolled himself up the wooden ramp to the deck and into the house.

Angel followed him with two bags.

Will brought up the rear, carrying the remaining parcels.

"Annette, you back yet?" Frank bellowed as he wheeled himself through the door and across the den toward the kitchen.

"I saw her waiting in the lift line to go to the top. That was about twenty minutes ago," Angel said. "She said she was making one last run down the Chute."

"Just like always," Frank muttered, "thinking only of herself, leaving all the work for me to do."

Kelly traded looks with Jeff. It made her nervous when Frank got in one of his moods. She didn't know why someone as sweet and optimistic as Annette would marry a man like him. Sometimes he scared Kelly.

Apparently, she wasn't the only one spooked by Frank's moodiness. Nathan, she noticed, was steering a wide course around him. Maybe he was thinking about the knife Frank had threatened Troy and Jeremy with. Being in a confined area like a kitchen, with plenty of knives around, probably didn't seem like a great idea.

Kelly and Angel started putting away the groceries while the other kids left to change clothes.

Kelly opened the refrigerator and put a gallon of milk on the top shelf. A loud shout came from the boys' room.

Frank spun his chair around and glared irritably at the swinging doors separating the kitchen from the den.

Angel smiled apologetically at him. "I think Nathan is a little hyper tonight. He gets that way sometimes, poor thing."

A second later, both Nathan and Chris tore into the kitchen. Nathan's face looked paler than the refrigerator door. His eyes were lemur-round, glittering with fear.

Chris stared at Kelly, his mouth working uselessly, his eyes blink-blinking and shockingly white against his dark skin.

"Keep it down, boys!" Frank barked. "You don't have to enter every room like an army storming a city."

"Mr. Riley, sir," Chris burst out. "There's a b-b-b-body in . . . " He jabbed his thumb in the direction of the bedroom. "Paula," he whispered hoarsely, "she's dead."

Riley stared at Chris as if he were speaking in a foreign language. "Young man, this isn't something to joke around about."

"I-I'm not joking, sir," Chris's voice rose an octave higher. "Honest—"

"He's not," Nathan seconded, staring intently at Frank. "Paula's lying on the floor in there. There's blood all around her. Looks like she's been stabbed."

Kelly guessed what Nathan must have been thinking. "Frank wouldn't do anything like that!" she cried, tearing out of the kitchen. "Paula can't be dead. I just talked to her a few hours ago!"

For the first time in over a year, she'd felt okay about Paula. Kelly began to believe she could forgive her—because she'd finally realized how deeply they shared the pain of Brian's loss. In a way, they'd changed from enemies to sisters in just a few hours.

Kelly prayed the boys were wrong.

She raced across the den, knocking aside Will and Jeff, who were hanging outside of the boys' bedroom door, peering inside as if unsure what to do.

Maybe Paula was just wounded, like Nathan had been, Kelly reasoned. Maybe if they got the bleeding stopped and called for an ambulance—

Kelly stopped short, just inside the bedroom door. Paula lay a few feet in front of her, twisted on her side. The wound in the center of her chest was a brownish red; it no longer bled. Paula lay still, so still that Kelly had to admit to herself the shallowest of breaths couldn't be entering her body.

Her eyes dropped to Paula's hand. In it lay what looked like a vegetable paring knife.

Jeff stepped up behind Kelly. "She's killed herself."

No, Kelly thought instinctively, *no, she didn't.* But she couldn't have said why . . . yet.

6

Kelly sat tucked up into a tight ball on the couch in the den, feeling the hate boil up inside of her again. This time it was a different kind of hate—one without a name or face attached to it.

She'd wished for more than three hundred nights that it had been Paula who'd drowned instead of Brian. The deep, aching anger she'd nurtured toward Paula was all she'd had to cling to for comfort. If Brian was gone, it had to be because someone evil and selfish had taken him from her. Paula was the obvious one to blame.

But yesterday she'd made her peace with Paula and with herself. She'd finally felt if she could leave the tragedy of Brian's drowning behind her and return to enjoying all of the things she loved—school, acting in the drama club productions, going out with Jeff for pizza or a movie.

She'd even started to like Paula, at least a little.

But the horror had returned, and this time she wished she had a face to give it, because then she could at least scream out her rage. Who had murdered Paula Schultz?

Frank had already called the police by the time Annette returned to the cabin. Two Garrett County police officers, a man and a woman, arrived within ten minutes. They went directly into the boys' bedroom, while the ski club members sat in the den in front of the fire and waited for them to do whatever ghastly inspection cops did at a murder scene. A moment later, the man crossed the den and walked out the front door without a word.

Kelly could hear him talking loudly through the door and figured he was radioing a report of what they'd found. One dead teenager.

No one talked in the den. No one moved around. Once in a while, somebody glanced at the open bedroom door, then quickly away, as if afraid of seeing what they all knew lay on the floor.

Kelly wrapped her arms around herself and shivered. Jeff pulled her over and pushed her head gently down on his shoulder. "Everything will be all right," he whispered.

No, she thought, *I don't think it will.* Her skin was so numb, she couldn't even feel his fingers on the back of her neck.

Kelly looked up out of her thoughts at the sound of sobbing. Angel and Isabel were hugging each other, crying. Nothing Chris was whispering to them seemed to calm them down.

Nathan sat glumly off by himself, chain smoking.

From the kitchen erupted choked half-whispers. Annette and Frank had retreated there as soon as the police arrived.

". . . my fault too?"

"It was your decision!"

Kelly shut out their squabbling and looked at Will. He was sitting on the floor two feet from the fire, staring into the flames. *He's in shock,* she thought. *A couple of hours ago, he was kissing her.*

Frank's wheelchair banged through the swinging door and into the den. Annette chased after him as he wheeled himself in an erratic circle, his face an explosive red, veins standing out on his forehead.

"Maybe it is your fault!" Frank bellowed. "That girl was obviously unstable . . . ready to go over the edge. And what do you do? You ask her to bunk with us! God knows, she might have turned that knife on one of the other kids or us!"

"Oh right," she groaned, "like I might as well have said, 'Here, make yourself at home. You can bump yourself off in our cozy cabin!'"

"Stop it!" Kelly shrieked, clapping her hands over her ears.

Annette came to a halt in the middle of the room and stared at her, a sheepish expression creeping across her face. Even Frank looked a little ashamed of himself.

"I'm sorry," Annette whispered. "We shouldn't be fighting, now of all times." She looked at her husband.

He turned away from her.

Then things started happening so fast it was hard to follow what was going on. Three additional police vehicles arrived. A man who looked like a doctor, carrying a small metal valise, strode through the den ahead of two other men, one carrying a camera, the other with a slightly larger case than the first man.

There was a muffled discussion behind the closed bedroom door, then the sounds of people moving around in the room, doing things in a very businesslike way. One of them must have cracked a joke. The others chuckled.

Kelly felt sick to her stomach. Death was routine for them, even at a remote place like Deep Creek Lake, but it was horrid and ugly and cruel to her.

An ambulance arrived—no siren wailing, no hurry since the passenger was already dead. A few minutes later, attendants took Paula away in a zippered bag. Kelly caught a glimpse of black plastic as the gurney rolled through the den. She buried her face in her palms, unable to watch.

And all the time hate and frustration simmered inside of her. Simmered, and boiled, and brewed.

Footsteps came from the boys' bedroom. The late-comer cops strode across the den and out the door, without ever looking at the group seated there, waiting tensely.

Kelly glanced up at the old wooden-cased clock on the wall. It was 1:45 a.m. She wondered if people in the surrounding cabins had been wakened by the police cruisers and ambulance. Were Troy and Jeremy peering through their cabin window, trying to figure out what might be going on?

The remaining two cops planted themselves in the middle of the room and looked around at the students, as if they were observing animals in a zoo. One was a squat man with rumpled hair and pants belted too high. He looked a lot like a guy Kelly had seen delivering pizzas in her neighborhood—not very coplike.

The woman seemed older than her partner, fortyish, about the age of Kelly's father. On TV the women cops usually were gorgeous. This one had plain tan eyes, and the lines in her face seemed too sharp. She wore no makeup. Whatever figure she might have had was hidden within a loose-fitting uniform.

"I'm Officer Margaret Shellborn. This is Officer Lawrence Baxter. Mr. Riley here told us the young lady we just removed was your guest. He also reported that you all had just returned from skiing and shopping to find her dead." Her voice was clipped and official sounding, but a pronounced southern drawl seeped through her words.

Will and Angel nodded. The rest of the group remained motionless and silent.

"To your knowledge was the girl alone in the cabin when this happened?" the pizza delivery cop asked.

Kelly noticed he didn't say, *When she killed herself.* So the police weren't taking for granted that

57

it was suicide. *Good,* she thought. *Give me a face to hate.*

"Most of us were out skiing," Kelly said tightly. "Nathan went for a walk. Mr. Riley drove into town for groceries."

Officer Shellborn nodded and wrote something on a clipboard. "And were all of you together the whole time you were skiing?" She looked at Kelly, as if she'd become official spokesperson by being first to volunteer information.

"Not really," Kelly admitted. "Some of the time I was with Jeff, my boyfriend." She nodded toward him, and he sat up straighter on the couch. "We had a little argument, though, and I skied by myself for while."

"How good of a skier are you?" the woman asked.

"Double black diamond," Jeff muttered.

The lady cop lifted an eyebrow and looked impressed, as if she knew what that meant.

But Kelly winced. Apparently Jeff was still angry with her for telling him to mind his own business when it came to her diet. "We sometimes ski together and sometimes alone, or meet up with other people," she said.

"Unless you meet up with a snowbank," Angel interrupted with a nervous giggle. "I saw you from another trail yesterday."

Kelly blushed. "Well, I sort of like . . . crashed. At any rate," she went on quickly, "after that I met up with Troy and Jeremy, and—"

"Are they here now?" Shellborn asked, half of her page already full of notes.

"No," Will said. "They're from another school and have a separate cabin. But they were over here before." He looked meaningfully at both cops.

"Yes?" Shellborn said.

"Those two punks broke in here and were looting

58

the cabin when I caught them red-handed!" Frank broke in.

"We don't *know* that," Annette said quickly. "In fact, they had a very good explanation for why they were here. And they seemed like very nice boys."

"What was their explanation?" Baxter asked.

Annette filled in the police officers, then the woman cop started asking each member of the ski club where he or she had been between 7 p.m., when night skiing started, and 11 p.m., when Paula's body had been discovered. People shouted out their locations and times, and Shellborn wrote frantically for a while, then looked up from her pad and held one hand in the air as if bringing traffic to a halt at a busy intersection.

"Whoa! This is getting pretty complicated. Sounds like you all were spread out over the whole mountain." She looked at Annette. "You really have no way of knowing where any of these kids were, do you?"

Annette glared at her. "If you're implying that I was neglecting my duty as a chaperon—"

"I wasn't saying that at all," Shellborn assured her. "I just said you can't be sure about times and places for anyone but yourself. So we'll need to speak to each of your students, separately."

Kelly didn't like the sound of that. "What you really mean is, you want to see if our stories fit. You think one of us might lie about where we were."

"You have no reason to lie, do you?" Shellborn fixed her with a firm tan gaze.

Kelly lifted her chin and met the woman's eyes. "Of course not."

"Good. And maybe no one else has a reason either."

Or maybe they do, Kelly thought with a shudder. *Maybe someone in this room killed Paula tonight.*

Shellborn looked at her watch, then glanced at

her partner. "It's after four o'clock. This bunch looks pretty beat. We'd better get started taking statements."

"Right," he said.

Shellborn turned to Frank and Annette. "We'll take over the girls' bedroom to use for interviews."

The two police officers talked to Annette and Frank first. In the meantime, Kelly sat at the kitchen table with Jeff, Chris, and Isabel, impatiently waiting for her turn.

No one had much to say to each other. Kelly drank two cups of coffee down fast, and felt the caffeine go right to her head, pushing away the last traces of fog from her brain.

Isabel stood up and crossed to the refrigerator. She took out a half-gallon of cookies 'n' cream ice cream. Plucking a spoon out of a drawer, she sat down at the table and started eating out of the carton.

Kelly watched her. The sight of the rich ice cream turned her stomach.

"You're going to make yourself sick," Kelly said.

"I'll eat what I want," Isabel muttered. "Isn't that what *you* always say?"

Kelly blinked at the unusual bitterness in her friend's voice. "I was only trying to help, Izzy," she murmured.

"So am I."

Kelly felt a twinge of guilt. How many times had she told Isabel to get off her back when Isabel scolded her for not eating? She'd just done the same thing to Jeff the day before.

From out in the den, Kelly heard Will ask, "I guess all that stuff at the lake happened the winter before I came to Thomaston High?"

"Yeah, you really missed out on a good time,"

Nathan sneered. "But I guess this is the end of it, now that Paula's offed herself."

"I don't think she did any such thing," Angel stated.

Kelly sat up rigidly at the table, suddenly alert. Reaching out, she grabbed the corner of one door panel and held it open so that she could see into the den.

"Why not?" Nathan asked. "I mean, it don't take a genius to add two and two. She's got a knife in her hand and hole in her chest. Come on now!"

Will nodded solemnly. "I don't agree with Nathan on much. But it does look pretty clear cut."

Nathan slapped his knee, laughing loudly. "Clear cut . . . knife. Don't you love it!"

Kelly shot up out of her chair and rushed into the den. "You're sick, Nathan!" she screamed at him. "You don't even care that somebody has died, someone you knew! How can you joke at a time like this?"

"What do you want me to do?" he demanded. "Blubber all over the place like a girl?"

"He's still angry about last year," Angel said softly. "He was really scared of Paula, you know."

"I'm not scared of anyone!" Nathan objected.

"You sure looked it," Will said calmly. "When Paula came through that door yesterday, I thought you were going to puke. You turned greener than most toads I've seen."

"You'd be a little wired too, if some girl came after you with a hunting knife," Nathan grumbled. "If you ask me, she got what she deserved."

Kelly felt the anger boil up inside of her again. "Nathan, you're a creep, a heartless creep!" she hissed.

She knew if she stayed any longer in the room she'd certainly strangle him.

Kelly grabbed her coat from the hook beside the cabin door and ran outside. She jogged into the woods for a ways before pulling on the parka and zipping up. Then she marched on, swinging her arms hard, then harder and faster to force her heart to pump. If she worked hard enough at exerting herself, she wouldn't have the energy to think about a worm like Nathan.

Kelly half expected Isabel or Jeff would follow her. In a way, she hoped they would. Izzy always knew what to say to calm her down. Usually, all Jeff had to do was hold her hand, and she'd feel as if there was a way to beat any problem.

But how do you beat death? she thought. A sudden, overwhelming hopelessness overtook her. She sank to the snowy ground, letting her tears flow without trying to stop them.

At last Kelly felt cried out. She stood up, brushed the snow off of her jeans, and looked around, trying to figure out how far she'd come from the cabin. The woods were pretty thick here, but she should be okay if she just retraced her steps.

As she walked, her thoughts became clearer and seeded with a new sense of purpose.

Why was she so sure Paula hadn't killed herself? Why did she feel the same horrible doubt she'd felt when Brian had drowned and people suggested he'd planned his death?

Brian had been too down to earth, too logical for suicide. If anyone could have rationalized killing himself or herself, it would be someone like Paula. She was emotional, obsessively romantic, impulsive.

But when Kelly had talked to her just twenty-four hours ago, she'd seemed as if she finally had a grip on her life. She'd seemed *normal.* She was even flirting with Will, and that had seemed a healthy sign. She'd looked happy.

"Hey, wait up!"

Kelly turned around. It was Troy, without his sidekick, Jeremy. She stuck her hands in her pockets to warm them and waited for him to catch up with her.

"Where are you going?" Troy asked.

"Nowhere," she said. "I just needed to get some air."

He laughed at her, his brown eyes twinkling. "You've been outside every day, all day!"

She shook her head and bit down on her lower lip. "It's not that. The police are at our cabin."

"The police?" He looked more curious than surprised. "What are the police doing there?"

"A girl was stabbed. She's dead." It felt as if the words were coming out of someone else's mouth.

"You mean, she was *murdered*?"

"The police are investigating now. I don't think they're sure yet," Kelly admitted. "Some of the kids think she killed herself. It sure looks that way—a knife was in her hand. I just don't believe it."

Troy took her arm and pulled her along the path. "Keep walking or you'll get cold. Was it someone I know?"

"Paula. The one we saw on the lake with the flowers," Kelly said.

He nodded, still not looking terribly surprised.

They walked on through the woods, passing two other cabins that were nestled among pines on the hillside above the lake. Smoke billowed from their chimneys, scenting the air woodsy-sweet.

Troy looked at her sideways. "Since you don't think Paula killed herself, you must have an idea who did it."

Kelly frowned, puzzled by the tension in his voice. "Why should you care? You didn't even know Paula."

He shrugged. "Why shouldn't I care? If there's a killer running around loose in these woods, don't you think anyone would want to know it?"

"I guess," she murmured.

"So, any ideas?"

Kelly looked at him sharply. "Nathan told the cops about you and Jeremy."

Troy turned away, and she could no longer see his expression. "Did he really?"

"Yes. He told them how you guys broke in and claimed you were looking for Jeremy's goggles."

"We were."

"Maybe. Or maybe not. It could be that Frank Riley was right and you broke in to steal whatever you could find. The goggles might have been a convenient excuse."

Troy let out a dry laugh. "If you knew Jeremy better, you'd realize he couldn't tell a lie if his life depended on it. He'd have blurted out the truth, if we'd been doing anything illegal."

"What about you, Troy? Can you lie to save your own skin?"

Troy's eyes narrowed and a thin smile lifted the corners of his lips. "Some people will do almost anything to save their own skin. You have to watch out for that kind, Kelly."

She gulped and staggered to a stop on the path.

"Come on," he said quickly, "I'll walk you back to the cabin. We must have come at least a mile by now. It's not safe for you to be out here on your own—especially with a killer loose."

Shivering at his words, Kelly reluctantly began walking again. But she wasn't sure she felt any safer with Troy than on her own.

7

Jeff stood at the front window, looking out at the snowy woods. It looked so peaceful out there. Inside the cabin felt like a war zone.

His stomach was tied up in knots and sort of queasy—the way he got on his way to the dentist's office. From the girls' room, he could hear muffled voices. The two cops were still interviewing members of the group. The questions they'd asked him had made him nervous.

Jeff had supposed they'd ask about Paula's mood. Had she been depressed? Had he ever heard her talk about killing herself? Routine stuff for a suicide investigation—at least the way the cops did it on TV.

But the woman cop had wanted to know exactly where he'd been every minute of the day Paula had died, and why he hadn't skied with the other kids instead of staying on his own so much of the time, and how did he feel about Paula?

"Didn't she try to kill your girlfriend?" the guy cop asked.

"It's understandable for you to feel protective of Kelly," the woman said. Then she wanted to know what he would have done if Paula had tried to hurt Kelly again.

Did they suspect *him* of killing Paula? He couldn't get the awful possibility out of his head.

He'd hated when the ambulance had come and taken Paula away, zipped up in a plastic bag. He wondered why they did that—like she was a sandwich they had to keep fresh. The thought made him feel even sicker.

He waited for Kelly at the window, then sitting on the opposite end of the couch from Nathan. Kelly didn't come back. Officers Shellborn and Baxter came out of the bedroom after finishing their interviews with everyone else and asked for her.

"I'll go find her," Jeff volunteered. "She just went for a walk." He didn't tell them how long she'd been gone.

"We'll be back to talk to her," Shellborn said. Then she gave instructions to Annette that no one was to enter the boys' bedroom. They'd sealed it off with bright yellow tape the night before, and it was to stay that way.

The boys had slept in the den that night and would have to continue sleeping there until the police were finished with their crime scene investigation.

The more Jeff thought about Paula's death, the more he wondered if someone completely outside of the group might have killed her. He returned to the front window and stared through it, seeing nothing.

Sure, Nathan was scared of Paula, and still mad about what she'd done to him. But would he really kill her? Wasn't it more likely that Paula had come back alone to the cabin and surprised a thief? She might just have been in the wrong place at the wrong time.

Angel stepped up beside Jeff. "She'll be back soon," she said.

"Huh?"

"Kelly." She pointed toward the window. "You've been watching for her, right?"

"Yeah."

"She'll be back any minute. It's starting to rain. Come over by the fire and work on the jigsaw puzzle with us. It'll help the time pass. No one will be skiing until the rain stops anyway."

Jeff agreed she was probably right.

Half an hour later Kelly stepped through the door and into the cabin.

Jeff looked up from the blue-sky pieces of the Grand Canyon puzzle he'd been working on with Angel, Chris, and Isabel. Behind Kelly he could see a shadowy figure. He recognized the voice right away and jumped to his feet, feeling a wave of heat wash across his face.

Kelly said, "Thanks for walking me back. See you around." Then she closed the door and turned to face Jeff and the group.

"What are you all staring at?" she asked.

"Where have you been?" Jeff ground out.

"Walking. I told you that before I left."

"You didn't say you were going to meet anyone."

Kelly scowled at him and pushed past, pulling off her jacket. "I didn't go out to *meet* anyone. I just ran into Troy on a path and we started walking together."

Nathan snorted. "Sure."

Kelly glared at him. "Shut up. It's the truth."

"Seems sort of strange, your running into Troy twice in two days. You two are spending more time together than we are," Jeff commented.

He didn't care that he was making Kelly angry. He was angry himself and felt like having company.

"I don't want to fight," Kelly said with a tired sigh. She marched off into her room, slammed the door behind her, and stayed there the rest of the day.

Jeff woke before the sun was up the next day. His back ached from sleeping on the hard wood floor two nights in a row. He was in an instant rotten mood as soon as he remembered the fight he'd had with Kelly.

He decided that when she came out of the room this morning, he'd apologize to her, even if he wasn't totally sure he'd been in the wrong.

Jeff tottered sleepily into the kitchen. He filled the tea kettle with water and put it on the stove. While he waited for the water to boil, he looked in the refrigerator to see if there were enough eggs for an omelette. There was a full dozen.

He cracked three eggs into a plastic bowl, beat them with a fork, then cooked them while sipping on a cup of instant coffee. Before he could dish up the eggs, he heard a car rumble up the road that passed by the cabin.

Jeff peered out the window, wondering who was driving around the lake at six in the morning. A Garrett County cruiser pulled up out front.

Jeff set his coffee cup down and went to the front door. Will and Chris were still sound asleep on the floor. Nathan snored on the couch. Jeff stepped outside so he wouldn't wake them up.

Shellborn and Baxter climbed out of the car and started toward the cabin.

"Forget something?" Jeff asked.

"We didn't finish questioning y'all," Shellborn drawled matter of factly. "Did Miss Peterson return to the cabin after we left?"

"Yeah, just a few minutes after."

"Good, will you please tell her we need to speak with her?"

"I—well, she's asleep," Jeff stammered. "Everyone's asleep."

"Wake her up," Baxter said.

Jeff was surprised by the sharpness of the man's voice. "I don't think Kelly can tell you anything the rest of us haven't. She wasn't even here when Paula was killed. She was skiing."

"Maybe she was and maybe she wasn't," Baxter muttered.

Shellborn shot him a warning look, and it occurred to Jeff that she must outrank her partner. "We still need her statement," she said.

"Yeah sure." Jeff pushed open the door. "I'll get her."

The cops stayed out on the porch. Inside, Jeff crossed the den, stepping over and around Chris and Will and the mess of blankets and quilts they were sprawled on top of. Nathan rolled over and mumbled something into the couch cushions that sounded like, "No way, man. No way."

Jeff hesitated at the girls' door before knocking softly.

It cracked open immediately, and Angel peered through the opening. "I knew they'd be back," she whispered hoarsely, her eyes pinpoint bright and huge.

Jeff stared at her. There was no window facing the front of the cabin from the bedrooms. How had she known the police were at the front door?

"They want to talk to Kelly," he whispered. "Can you wake her up?"

"Sure."

He paced the floor then paused in front of Annette and Frank's door. Should he let their chaperons know what was going on?

Annette had looked exhausted by the time she'd told her students she was turning in the night before. And he'd heard Frank badgering her for another hour after they'd closed their door. He decided to let them sleep.

Kelly wasn't really asleep when Jeff came to her door. She'd been so upset by her fight with Jeff that she'd tossed and turned most of the night.

"Jeff isn't the jealous type," she'd told Isabel just after they'd turned off the lights. "I don't know why he's acting like such a jerk about Troy."

"He's not being a jerk," Isabel said. "He's worried about you."

"Why?"

"You don't know anything about Troy. He could be a real creep, dangerous even."

"I can take care of myself," Kelly assured her.

But Isabel's words had started Kelly wondering. What was it Troy had said about a person being willing to do almost anything to save his own skin? Had he been talking about himself? Kelly groaned. "I don't know, Jeff's just acting so weird lately."

"Maybe he has other things on his mind," Isabel whispered into the dark.

"Like what?"

"Like what all of us are thinking about: next year. We won't be in high school anymore. We'll all go our separate ways. Away from our old friends."

Kelly shook her head. "Brooding about next year doesn't sound like Jeff. He's been planning on going to college since elementary school. The day he was accepted at Harvard, he told me it was the happiest day of his life."

But her conversation with Izzy had been last night, and this morning as Kelly hurriedly finished dressing in jeans and a loose sweatshirt, she realized she was no longer angry with Jeff.

Vaguely, she realized that the denim waistband of her jeans gapped. She'd lost more weight, all of her clothes felt too loose. Her stomach growled,

70

begging to be fed, but she had too much on her mind to think about eating now.

Later, she thought, *I'll eat later.*

Stuffing her feet into unlaced athletic shoes, she crossed the den and stepped out onto the front porch where Jeff stood with the two cops. An icy blast of wind hit her, snatching away her breath. The frigid glares of the two police officers greeted her.

The woman cop nodded at the door and Jeff took the hint. "I'll wait inside so you guys can talk," he said.

Kelly wanted to reach out and touch him on the arm, to let him know she wasn't still angry with him. But he avoided making eye contact with her. Maybe it was too late to apologize. Kelly's heart broke a little more.

She turned to Shellborn. "It's cold, can't we talk inside?"

"This won't take long, and it's better if we have some privacy," the woman said, consulting her clipboard.

Kelly nodded. "Okay, but I don't really know anything."

They asked her to tell them in detail where she'd been throughout the day Paula had died. Kelly told them, as best as she could remember.

"Now, let's go back a little further," Shellborn suggested.

"How far back?" Kelly asked, thinking she meant the day before Paula had arrived.

"Back to November, your junior year."

The words felt like a hot knife cutting through the chilled butter of her soul. "You mean, back to the last time I was here. When Brian Lopez drowned."

"Yes." Shellborn studied her expression. "He was your closest friend."

71

Kelly nodded. "We'd known each other since elementary school. Third grade, I think. We talked about everything."

"What kinds of things?" Baxter asked.

Kelly thought for a minute. "Dating, schoolwork, the plays I was in with the drama club."

"So you felt a great loss when he died," Shellborn stated. Her eyes flickered for an almost unnoticeable instant to her partner, then back to Kelly.

"Yeah, sure. I was very upset about Brian."

"And how did you feel when you learned that his girlfriend, Paula, was responsible?"

Kelly's mouth suddenly felt dry. "I-I don't know. I've been thinking about that. I guess she was pretty upset too. I mean, she couldn't deal with it. That's why she tried to kill Nathan and me, because she couldn't admit what had really happened and she didn't want anyone to find out."

"Y'all hated Paula Schultz," the woman's honey-eyed drawl sugar-coated the accusing words.

Suddenly, Kelly no longer felt the cold air whistling around her. A fiery anger ignited in her chest and burned its way outward through her limbs.

"*Not* enough to kill her," Kelly blurted out, "or even want to hurt her."

"Come on now," Baxter chuckled, although he didn't sound amused. "That girl was responsible for your best friend's death. Everyone we've talked to said you were so torn up after it happened, you didn't crack a smile for months. You turned down a lead role in the spring play and didn't try out for the community theater production, like you had done the previous summer."

Kelly seethed. *This isn't fair!* she thought wildly. They'd been snooping around in her life. She was so furious, she couldn't force her mouth to work.

Shellborn took a turn. "What about Paula's attempt to kill you? She almost succeeded. You didn't hold a grudge against her? That would be natural."

Kelly wrapped her arms around her ribs to hold in her fury. The wind blew right through the soft fleece of her sweatshirt. She still felt as if she was burning up. "Paula attacked Nathan too," she finally choked out. "I don't see you grilling him in sub-zero temperatures."

"We've already questioned him. He has an alibi. Several witnesses saw him at the bar in the lodge."

Baxter smiled. "He was trying to get people to buy him drinks. Not exactly honorable behavior, but it is an alibi."

"Well, *I* have an alibi," Kelly said. "I was skiing."

"Who with?"

"By myself most of the time. Not many of the kids are able to ski black diamond trails."

"The rest of the time?"

Kelly thought for a moment. "I was with Jeff some. And I was with Troy."

Both cops seemed to react to that name, but it was with no more than a flicker of the eyelid.

"Have you questioned Troy and his friend Jeremy?" Kelly asked. "They broke into the cabin once before. Maybe they came back and—"

"They're clean," Baxter said, cutting her short.

"How do you know? How can you accuse me of killing Paula, then just dismiss the idea that someone who broke into the cabin could have done the same thing?"

Kelly hadn't stepped onto the porch intending to accuse anyone of murder, but now that the police seemed to be pointing the finger of guilt at her, she felt the need to remind them there were other possibilities.

"We're not accusing y'all of anything," Shellborn

73

said in a flat voice teachers use before they give detention. "We're just looking into motives. You seem to have a very strong one."

And a very weak alibi, Kelly thought. Not a good combination. She didn't know what to say. Suddenly, the heat of her own frustration and anger seeped away, leaving her feeling weak in the knees and out of breath and terribly cold.

"I didn't kill Paula," she stated. "I wouldn't do something like that, even if I did still blame her for Brian's death. And I didn't."

Shellborn studied her for a minute, then jammed her pen under the clipboard clamp. "We'll need to speak with your chaperon."

8

Kelly felt Jeff watching her from a chair beside the fireplace as she knocked timidly on Annette's bedroom door.

"I'd better speak with them alone," Annette said when Kelly told her the police wanted to see her.

Kelly wandered into the kitchen. A hollow place in her stomach cried out for food. But she knew she'd throw up if she tried to eat anything now.

Jeff followed her. "I'll make you some eggs and toast," he offered, moving toward the stove.

"No thanks." The thought of a raw egg—all runny and gelatinous—made her feel like gagging.

"I'm sorry about last night," he said. "It's up to you if you want to hang with some other guy."

Kelly sighed tiredly. "I told you, I hadn't planned on meeting up with Troy. He just showed up." She sat down at the table, and he sat in the chair across from her.

"He gets around."

"Huh?"

"I said, he sure gets around."

Kelly frowned, but decided Jeff didn't mean anything bad by his comment. He was just as confused as she was.

Then she really thought about what he'd just said. "You're right, Troy does get around. It's strange. I mean, he seems to spend more time around our cabin and with us than he does with the kids from his own school."

Jeff nodded. "Maybe he doesn't get along with them very well."

"Jeremy seems to like him."

"That dork? He'd probably follow anyone around who'd let him. He looks like a lost puppy." Jeff made a droopy hound-dog face.

Kelly laughed for the first time in what seemed like an eternity. "That's just how he looks!" Then something struck her that she hadn't considered before. "Have you ever noticed how Troy gets people talking about themselves?"

"I haven't been around him as much as you have."

"Cheap shot."

"Well, it's true." He reached for a handful of stale popcorn from a bowl that had been left out the night before. Munching thoughtfully, he added, "Maybe he's just a good listener."

"No," Kelly said. "It's more than just making small talk. I got the feeling when we were talking about what happened to Brian last year, he was fishing for information."

"What kind?"

"I don't know. Everything. He was almost too interested in everyone."

"Did you tell the police that?"

"No. I mean, it's just a feeling, nothing I can put a finger on."

"Well, I'm sure if he's up to anything they'll figure it out for themselves."

Kelly winced. "I'm not so sure. I think they've stopped looking for Paula's killer."

Jeff looked surprised. "Why? They buying the theory she killed herself?"

"No, they definitely suspect someone else killed her."

76

"Who?" He thrust another handful of kernels into his mouth.

"Me."

Bits of popcorn exploded from Jeff's mouth. He coughed loudly. "You?"

"Yes, me."

"You're imagining things. They're just acting suspicious of everyone."

Kelly dropped her head into her hands and closed her eyes. Her head hurt. Her stomach churned. She felt dizzy. When had she eaten last? The thought of food made her feel worse.

"They were asking all sorts of questions about Paula and Brian." She pressed a hand to her stomach. "Stuff like, wasn't I really angry and upset with Paula for what happened? I guess the other kids must have mentioned that Thanksgiving."

Jeff looked suddenly uneasy. "I did, but I never suggested you might have wanted to kill Paula."

Kelly sighed. "I'm sure you didn't."

The kitchen door swung open and Annette plodded in. Her face was pale, and her lips were a grayish-blue from the cold. "Is the water hot?" she asked, waving at the kettle on the stove.

Jeff jumped up. "I'll reheat it. Want some coffee?"

"Do you know how to make the real stuff? Nice and strong?"

"No sweat," he said, swinging wide the refrigerator door and pulling out the can of coffee grounds. From a nearby cupboard he took a carafe with an old-fashioned drip attachment. He scrambled around and found a cone-shaped paper filter in a drawer. "I worked one summer at a coffee house," he said. "I make unbelievable java."

Annette didn't seem to be listening to him. She sat limply in one of the chairs at the table. After a while she focused on Kelly. "I told them you weren't the kind of person to ever hurt anyone."

Kelly bit down on her bottom lip and pressed her palms against her thighs to stop her hands from shaking. "Am I going to be arrested?"

Annette shook her head. "It sounds to me as if they don't have enough evidence. It's mostly just your relationship with Paula and Brian that's convinced them you should be considered the primary suspect."

"Oh great," Kelly moaned.

"That's stupid!" Jeff burst out. "Anyone who knows Kelly, knows—"

"—how much I loved Brian," Kelly finished for him. "We were like brother and sister . . . only we didn't fight." She shook her head. "I can't believe this is happening."

"We're supposed to go home tomorrow," Jeff said. "You'll feel better back in your own house."

"I'm afraid that will have to wait," Annette murmured. She blew a strand of blonde hair out of her eyes. "The police have asked that we remain at Wisp until they tell us we're free to go home."

Nathan pushed through the café-style doors. "I heard that. Can you believe those Nazi types think they can order us around?" He looked a wreck. His hair was standing on end all over his head. He'd slept in his clothes, and a patchy, reddish-brown beard had grown in overnight. "There's nothing to do here anyway."

Annette looked at him. "You signed up for a ski trip. I haven't seen you skiing much."

"I signed up to get away from my old man," Nathan grumbled. "He was getting on my nerves."

"Then you should know what it's like being around you," Jeff muttered, pouring a mug of coffee for Annette.

Nathan glared at him. "I'm not stupid, you

know. I can figure out when you're trashing me. Hey, is there enough in that thing for me?"

Jeff filled two more mugs to the brim, for himself and Nathan. He looked at Kelly, but she shook her head.

"So, we all have to stay at Wisp because of me," she said.

"Well, let's just say, we stay until the police figure out who they're really after." Annette smiled dimly at her.

Kelly squeezed her eyes shut. It didn't block out what was happening. It didn't help at all.

She felt someone touch her hand, then pick up her fingers from where they lay on the table, and she smiled. She knew Jeff's touch. Even that little gesture made her feel somewhat better.

"What are you thinking?" he asked.

"I can't let anyone believe I did something this terrible," she said firmly.

"You can't help what people think," Jeff said.

"He's right," Annette whispered.

"No, but I can prove they're wrong."

"Yeah right," Nathan muttered into his coffee. "Like, how?"

"By finding out who really did kill Paula," she said.

Annette observed her over the rim of her mug. "Kelly, it's not your place to play detective. Let the police do their jobs. They'll eventually realize you're not a violent person, and they'll find the real person . . . if there is a person."

"How could there not be a person?" Kelly asked.

"Yeah, like it might have been aliens from another galaxy," Nathan chuckled.

"Of course not," Annette snapped, losing her patience with him. "As much as I hate to think of the possibility, suicide still hasn't been ruled out. Paula might have stabbed herself with that knife.

79

After all, she'd played around with the idea of killing herself before. Her boyfriend died trying to talk her out of doing it once before."

"I suppose," Kelly said. But no matter how many times she thought about that possibility, it still seemed wrong.

By mid-morning the weather had become overcast and the temperature was dropping. A lot of skiers took to the mountain, hoping to beat bad weather that was reported heading north from West Virginia. If the storm was snow, it would be welcome. If it turned to rain there might not be any more skiing that spring.

One skier crossed the nearly deserted snack bar in the lodge to the pay phones in a rear corridor, then waited for a girl to finish using the telephone in an old-fashioned booth. There were two other ordinary phones out in plain sight. But the booth made if far more difficult for anyone to listen in on a conversation.

The caller punched in 1, then an area code and seven more digits. Someone picked up the phone on the other end in the middle of the second ring.

"I've got a problem," the caller said. "I don't know when I can get that shipment to you. Things have gotten pretty hot all of a sudden."

"Define *pretty hot*," a gravelly voice said.

"Some girl got herself dead."

"So, how does that affect you?"

"It means there are cops crawling all over this stupid mountain. I can't move the stuff until they clear out."

"How long will that be?"

"I don't know. With luck, not long. They seem to think one of her friends, another girl, did it."

There was a pause, then measured breathing

from the other end. The caller waited, hoping that meant the boss was pleased.

"This girl the cops think did it . . . she didn't kill her, did she?"

"Hey, there was an old grudge of some kind and—"

"Don't lie to me!" Apparently he wasn't happy.

"There was. Honest."

"I don't mean that, idiot. I mean, *she* didn't kill that girl. You did."

"Me? I wouldn't—"

"Lie to the cops, not to me!" barked the voice.

"You're right," the caller admitted reluctantly. This was one man no one dared cross. "I killed her. But I had to or she would have spoiled everything. She'd have blabbed to her shrink about me, and it would have come out . . . what I do for you guys."

"*How* would that have come out?"

I've said too much, the caller thought, feeling suddenly a little desperate. A thin line of sweat trickled down the side of his neck. But there was no turning back.

"Somehow . . . well, someone would tie us together—you and me. Of course I'd never rat on you. But it would get out. She had a big mouth and she was a screwy girl."

"That was still a dumb thing to do, kill her."

"It would have been dumber to let her walk away with what she knew."

"I suppose," the voice admitted grudgingly.

Maybe it hadn't been such a bad mistake after all.

"One more thing," the voice added.

"Yeah, boss."

"This girl the cops think did it? Make sure they keep on thinking that way. If they change their minds, they might start looking in another direction. I don't want them looking anywhere near me."

"You've got nothing to worry about. Nothing." But when the caller hung up, the hand that had been holding the receiver was shaking.

The day seemed to drag by. Kelly didn't feel much like skiing, even when the clouds parted for a few hours. Then the rains started and most of the group changed out of their ski togs and hung out at the cabin. Chris and Jeff hiked half-heartedly up to the lodge to check out the trail conditions, but they didn't bother taking equipment along and they were back in less than an hour, drenched to the skin.

When the rain turned from steady to a torrential downpour around noon, the lifts closed and everyone started complaining.

"I can't believe our rotten luck," Chris muttered. "Rain on a ski holiday . . . and the weather report predicts more tomorrow."

"Gee," Will whispered in Kelly's ear, "I sure wish you hadn't offed your old friend. We'd be out of here by now."

Kelly glared at him.

Nathan overheard. "Don't listen to him, Kel! Old Paula had it coming. You remember how it was, even if everyone else forgets." His eyes darkened and narrowed, fixing on the past. "Nearly ripped my guts out. Serves her right."

"Don't say that!" Kelly choked out. She sank lower into the couch cushions. "Paula didn't deserve to die—and I didn't kill her."

The rain drummed on the den's windows. Even though Will had stoked up a roaring blaze in the fireplace, a terrible chill filled the room.

Nathan fidgeted around in the chair and shot an anxious look toward the boys' bedroom.

"You can't go in there," Kelly reminded him.

Will nodded. "The cops will freak out. It's called tampering with evidence, my friend."

"I'm not going in there," Nathan snapped, but he couldn't keep his eyes off of the door.

"What you leave in there?" Will asked, looking curious. "Your booze? Drugs? You'd think the cops would have already found his supply, right?"

"Leave him alone," Jeff said. "We're all a little edgy."

Will laughed. "He's a total pothead. He can't leave the stuff alone, but he can't figure out how to get to it."

"Maybe he's worried about something else in there," Isabel commented, observing the door solemnly.

"What's that supposed to mean?" Nathan demanded.

"Nothing . . . it's nothing," Isabel stared at her hands.

Kelly sat up slowly. Had she imagined the tension in Izzy's voice? "*I* didn't kill Paula. If you know something that helps prove it, please tell me."

"I-I don't know anything," Isabel said softly. "I just couldn't help wondering why Nathan looked so nervous about the boys' room. Like Will said, he could be hiding something in there."

Nathan shrugged. "Big deal. I just like a drink now and then. Everyone has at least one bad habit."

"Difference is, Nate old man, you've got 'em all!" Will burst out with a laugh. "Every last one of 'em."

"Shut up, Will. You're making things worse," Jeff growled. He turned to Isabel. "Go on with what you were saying."

"Well, he could be hiding stuff he didn't want

Annette or Frank to see, like booze or dope. Or he could be nervous because. . . ." Isabel hesitated and chewed her bottom lip.

Kelly leaned forward, her nerves pricking beneath her skin. "What is it, Izzy?"

"Because he left something behind he hadn't intended to when he . . . I mean, *if* he killed Paula." Her voice crackled then dropped off to a whisper at the end.

The silence in the room was thick and dark, like molasses on a winter day, and no one dared speak.

At last Nathan let out a sharp crack of a laugh and stood up from the couch. "You're all crazy. I'm not hanging around to listen to any more of this junk you guys are dreaming up."

He grabbed his parka from the hook on the wall and swung around to face the cabin door.

"Wait, Nathan!" Angel cried, jumping up to head him off. "It's pouring out there. You'll get freezing wet!"

"Better wet than dumped on by my so-called friends!"

He slammed his way out through the door. Angel turned and looked reproachfully at the group. "That wasn't very nice of all of you."

Kelly stood up, crossed the room, and pulled down her own coat. "It might not have been nice, but if Nathan killed Paula, *I* don't intend to take the blame."

"Where are you going?" Jeff asked, when she started putting on her coat.

"Nathan gave me an idea."

"What?" Isabel asked.

"I'm going to see if I can find out who might have wanted Paula dead."

"That's much more positive thinking," Angel commented, looking pleased. "I'll go with you to help."

"Want me to come too?" Jeff asked.

Kelly thought for a second then shook her head. "Having a crowd around won't help me do what I have in mind. But you and a couple of the other guys could go around to neighboring cabins and ask if anyone's seen anybody who looks suspicious in the woods around the cabins in the last few days. You know, someone who doesn't seem to belong."

"They might have had a break-in too," Jeff pointed out. "Like you said before, maybe Paula surprised a thief and he panicked."

"Right," Kelly said. She hoped that was what had happened. It would mean none of them were to blame—except maybe Troy and Jeremy.

"I'll go with Jeff," Chris said.

"Is there any other way I can help?" Isabel asked.

Kelly zipped up her coat and pulled on a pink knit ski cap and matching mittens. "I don't think so. It would probably be a good idea if you stayed here in case the police come back. Then you can tell them where we are."

Jeff and Chris decided to start questioning the residents of cabins nearest to theirs, then spread out in a circle. Kelly and Angel headed down the hill in the opposite direction.

"Where are we going?" Angel asked, smiling dreamily at the raindrops freezing on the pine tree branches overhead. She seemed to enjoy being outside, even in the worst weather.

"To the lodge," Kelly said. "I want to make some phone calls."

9

Kelly held her breath and listened as the phone number she'd dialed rang a hundred miles away in Thomaston, Maryland. Angel stood beside her, twirling a strand of blonde hair and humming as she waited. They were standing outside, at a pay phone between the parking lot and the woods. She'd have rather used the phone booth inside, where it was warm, but some boy was hogging it, calling what seemed like an endless stream of girlfriends.

On the fifth ring a man's voice answered. "The Schultz residence, may I help you?"

She still wasn't sure what she was going to say. Had the police said anything to the Schultzes about their suspicions? "Um, I'd like to talk to Mrs. Schultz, please."

"She's not able to come to the phone. There's been a family tragedy and she's—"

"I know," Kelly interrupted. "That's why I'm calling. I'm a friend of Paula's. I was with her just a few hours before she died. I'm trying to find out what happened to her."

There was a moment of silence then, "Young lady, if you were a close friend of my niece, you'd know she had a lot of emotional problems. Suicide was her most recent."

"But she didn't kill herself!" Kelly shouted into the receiver, sensing the man was about to hang up on her. "Please, listen to me. Even the police don't think it was suicide. They think she was murdered."

In the background were the muffled sounds of voices followed by crackling air, as if the uncle had covered the receiver with his hand.

"Did they hang up?" Angel asked.

"Not yet," Kelly said. But she expected he might at any moment.

"Kelly, is that you?" a woman's voice quavered in her ear.

Kelly tightened her grip on the phone. "Yes, Mrs. Schultz."

"Are you . . . are you all right, dear?"

After the incident with Paula last year, the Schultz's had seemed almost grateful when things turned out as they had. Their daughter was in a hospital instead of prison. And no one had sued them.

"I'm fine, Mrs. Schultz. I just want you to know I'm very sorry about Paula. We hadn't seen each other in a long time. Then she showed up at Deep Creek Lake and we had a chance to talk. She seemed a lot better."

Mrs. Schultz cleared her throat. "I had thought she was. Paula acted much more together, if you know what I mean." She paused. "But a few nights ago, she ran away from the hospital, and no one knew where she'd gone. Dear, I just feared something terrible would happen."

Kelly blinked in surprise. "She left the hospital without permission? Her doctor didn't give her permission to come up here to the lake?"

"My, no! Whatever gave you that idea?"

"Paula told me that coming back here was part of her treatment."

Mrs. Schultz sighed as if she were in pain. "I'm afraid that must have been all in her imagination. I wish someone had known what she had in mind so that we could have stopped her." A distant clicking sound came over the phone as if the woman were drumming her nails over the receiver. "You told my brother the police don't believe it was suicide? I don't understand."

"They think—" Kelly decided it wouldn't be a good idea to tell her that *she* was the chief suspect. "They think someone else did it."

"No one has said anything to us."

"Maybe they have to be sure. You know, find the proper evidence and all."

"Probably," Mrs. Schultz said. Her words sounded washed over and blurred, like when you add too much water to fingerpaints and they bleach out on the paper. Kelly knew she was crying now. "Kelly dear, I know this might sound selfish, but I really do hope you're right. I hate to think that Paula was so desperately sad she could think of no other solution but death."

"If it makes you feel any better," Kelly said, softly, "when Paula and I talked the day she died, she told me she'd come to the lake to say her final goodbye to Brian and put all of that behind her. She sounded happy. She was acting like her old self— flirting with a boy, listening to music with us, talking with the other kids about maybe going to college."

Mrs. Schultz let out a choked sob. "Oh God, my poor little girl—"

Kelly swallowed. Maybe she'd made things worse instead of better.

"I'm sorry," Mrs. Schultz said at last. "Thank you for telling me. It really does make me feel much better. I want to remember her as being happy, if just for a little while."

Kelly looked at Angel, who was conversing with a squirrel on a tree limb above her head. "There's just one thing before I go," Kelly said. "I need to know if Paula's had any serious trouble with anyone at home or at the hospital."

"Trouble? What kind of trouble?"

"I don't know really. I just wondered if someone might have been angry enough with her to want to hurt her. If so, they could have followed her up here."

"Not that I know of. She never spoke of any arguments or problems with patients or staff at the hospital. And the only contact she had with people in Thomaston was with her family, when we visited her."

Other patients at a mental hospital, Kelly thought. She nodded, although the woman couldn't see her. "Okay, thanks. I thought it might be worth a try."

"If I think of anything," Mrs. Schultz said, "I'll call you."

Kelly gave her the phone number of the rental office. Since many of the more rustic cabins were still without telephones, the office took messages for vacationers.

"Oh, one more thing . . . Did Paula have a car to drive?"

"Why, no." The woman sounded puzzled. "Why would she as long as she was living at the hospital?"

"Right. Thanks." Kelly said goodbye and hung up, then stood staring at the phone.

"No luck, huh?" Angel asked, waving goodbye to her friend in the tree.

"No." Kelly thought for a minute. "But I have another idea."

They walked back to the lodge and Kelly found a sign for the Visitor Services office. She wanted to find out the ways a person might come to Wisp, if they didn't have a car. There weren't any taxis this far away from the cities.

"Paula must have either hitched a ride or taken a bus from Baltimore to get to Wisp," Kelly reasoned. "If it was a bus, maybe someone saw her."

"Or got off with her," Angel suggested, her eyes sparkling as if she were enjoying herself.

Kelly nodded. "Right."

But when they asked the clerk at the desk if they could see a list of passengers who might have come in early on the day Paula died, the woman looked at them as if they were wasting her time.

"It's very important," Kelly insisted.

The clerk looked unimpressed and puffed twice on her cigarette before answering. "Well, it doesn't matter how important it might be, because I wouldn't have that information anyway. Only Trailways keeps a record of their ticket sales. You'll have to contact them."

"How?" Kelly asked.

The woman shoved a timetable across the desk at her. "There's an 800 number."

They returned to the telephone. Kelly took another quarter out of the fanny pack she'd strapped around her waist to carry her wallet. She dialed and when the operator came on the line explained what she needed.

"We're not allowed to give out that sort of information over the telephone," the operator said.

Kelly hung up.

"What's wrong?" Angel asked.

"The woman won't give out names of passengers over the phone. I need people's names and where they got off."

Angel laid her head to one side and studied her fingernails, painted a pearly white to match her wardrobe. "Let me try. Dial again, but hang up if it's the same person."

Kelly didn't think any amount of sweet talking from Angel would persuade a bus company employee to choke up private information, but she punched in the numbers anyway.

She had to try twice before getting a man's voice. Quickly, she handed the receiver to Angel.

"This is Officer Margaret Shellborn of the Garrett County police," Angel said, sounding very official, in a nearly perfect imitation of the woman police officer's voice. "We need information about a young woman who might have been one of your passengers."

Kelly stifled a laugh and held her breath, sure the person on the other end would refuse her. Miraculously, Angel continued talking, then nodding, talking, then nodding.

Kelly was so excited she could hardly breathe. She pressed her ear close to Angel's trying to hear the speaker's next answers. But a crowd of kids passing by were talking and laughing loudly, and Kelly couldn't hear over them.

Angel hung up.

"What happened?" Kelly asked.

"Paula was definitely on an early morning bus the day you met her at the lake. She used a student ID to get a discounted fare. They keep records of that sort of sale. The bus came from Baltimore and made stops at Frederick and Cumberland before reaching Wisp."

"So, who else got off at this stop?"

"No one. Just Paula."

Kelly sighed, disappointed. It had seemed as if they'd been getting somewhere. Now they had little more than when they'd started.

"Sorry," Angel said. "I tried."

"That's okay. Come on, let's head back to the cabin and see if the boys turned up anything."

Although the rain had slowed for a while, it was coming down harder now. The girls pulled their hoods over their heads and trudged across the slushy snow. Kelly's jacket was beginning to soak through, and she felt chilled. The path from the lodge at the base of the mountain to the cabins that were scattered over the wooded hillside was narrow and slippery. The sky was so dark, it felt as though night were closing in around them as they moved through the trees, although it was the middle of the day.

No one else was on the path or in sight around the cabins they passed. Kelly imagined disgruntled skiers huddling in front of their fireplaces, grumbling about the weather. But at least they were toasty warm and dry in front of their cozy blazes. For all the information she'd gotten, she might as well have stayed inside too, she thought glumly.

They were deep into the woods when a sound off to one side of the path made Kelly jump.

"What was that?" she asked, grabbing Angel's arm.

Angel stopped and listened. "I don't hear anything."

Kelly looked around. Rough brown tree trunks and low, prickly brush surrounded them. Nothing moved between the branches. Yet she was sure something *had* moved. It wasn't just the wind that had made that rustling, crunching sound.

"I guess it was just an animal," she murmured doubtfully.

They continued on, but it wasn't long before Kelly started noticing that the sounds their own feet made along the soft ground weren't creating the snapping-twig sounds she heard off to their right. She didn't say anything to Angel but she was sure someone was following them—watching them or perhaps waiting for the right moment to . . .

To what?

She had a vision of Paula's body, lying in a pool

of blood. Then the face altered—first the nose, then the mouth, and the eyes opened . . . they were no longer Paula's blue, but had become a familiar vivid green. It was as if the transformation was happening through animation magic, and she was suddenly looking at her own face, cartoonishly grotesque. And the body in the blood was hers.

Kelly's breath slid in and out of her lungs, in short, fast puffs. She calculated that it was another half mile back to the cabin. The sounds seemed to be getting closer. Suddenly, Angel stopped walking. She screwed up her face and glared at the woods.

"Don't make so much noise!" she hissed, as if scolding a small child in a library.

Kelly stared at her. "I'm not making noise."

"I'm not talking to you. I'm talking to *them*."

"Them?" Kelly stared at Angel. Did she *know* who was following them?

"Yes. They're usually much more considerate."

Kelly stared between the tree trunks. Shadows shifted and retreated in the gray rain. But she still could see nothing moving.

She took Angel firmly by the arm and walked her along the path, more scared than ever. "What's out there?" she whispered hoarsely in Angel's ear.

"Don't you know?"

"This isn't funny, Angel. You're supposed to be helping, not scaring the stuffing out of me!"

"Oh, I didn't mean to scare you." Angel slipped free and stopped in the middle of the path to observe her with a sympathetic, almost motherly expression. "It's just your guardian, looking after you."

Kelly let out a lengthy breath of exasperation and squinted at Angel. "My guardian? As in guardian angel?"

Angel beamed. "Sure."

With a groan, Kelly started walking again.

Angel ran to catch up with her. "Are you angry with me?"

"No, I'm not angry. I just wish you wouldn't start this crazy stuff right now. I have enough to worry about—like getting thrown into prison for the rest of my life." Kelly pressed a hand to her stomach. It was pinching terribly; she really should eat something.

Angel giggled. "Oh, that won't happen, Kelly. You're too nice a person to end up in jail or the electric chair or anything like—"

"Quit it!" Kelly warned. "I mean it. This is reality, Angel. The police think I killed Paula. Unless I can prove someone else did it, I'm sunk. There are no angels!"

Angel pursed her lips and observed her sadly. "If you have no faith, it's much harder for them to help you."

"Good grief!" Kelly groaned and started walking faster.

She was sure she was being watched. Watched and followed. And the feeling didn't go away as they worked their way further up the hillside into denser pine trees and brush.

But their shadow's presence, whoever or whatever it might be, didn't seem to bother Angel in the least. She tagged along, humming to herself as she strolled lazily through the woods.

"Come on! Run!" Kelly shouted. She broke into a jog, hoping Angel would finally come to her senses and make a break for it too.

Branches swept past her, and her chest ached and her head pounded as if she were striking it against a rock. Although the air around her was cold and wet, sweat trickled down the crease of her spine, inside her clothing.

At last she could see the cabin. It was only a

hundred yards or so ahead. Annette and her friends would be there. She'd be safe from whatever was chasing her . . . for now she was sure that she hadn't left it behind by running. "It" had kept pace with her. If her senses didn't lie, it was closing in on her.

Kelly ignored the pain in her head and stomach and desperately plunged forward. A few feet ahead of her, a shadow shot out from behind a tree and stopped in her path. Kelly ran straight into a muscled body, and the strong arms latched around her, holding her tightly.

10

Kelly let out a shriek and pulled away so violently, the arms slipped from around her.

"Hey, hold on! What's the rush?"

Looking up in shock, she staggered backwards a couple of steps before regaining her balance. Kelly brushed rust-colored wisps of hair out of her eyes beneath her cap. "Troy! Oh geez. It's you."

"Yeah. Are you okay? You look terrible."

"I'm fine . . . no, I'm not." Kelly tried to catch her breath. "Someone has been following me through the woods. I was so scared, I started running." She looked questioningly at him.

"Hey, don't get any crazy ideas. It wasn't me. I just stopped by your place to find out how you guys were doing. I talked to your chaperons and was on my way back to my own cabin when I heard you crashing through the woods." He smiled at her. "Then you crashed into me, which was a nice surprise."

"You were hiding behind that tree," she said accusingly.

"Hey, when you're in the middle of a forest and you hear something thrashing around in the brush, you're cautious, if you're smart. I thought you might be a bear or something."

"Well, I'm not a bear, and I don't appreciate you leaping out at me like that."

Troy laughed. "If I hadn't leaped out you wouldn't have stopped. I wanted to talk to you."

From a distance, a mystical humming sound echoed through the woods.

Troy turned and stared into the trees. "What on earth is that?"

"I'm not sure it is *on earth*," Kelly said dryly. "That's Angel, communing with the spirits or something."

"Huh?"

"You'll see."

Angel skipped between the trees along the slushy path. She didn't seem to be aware of the icy rain still falling, or that the long hems of her white dress were dragging soggily along the ground. She smiled sunnily when she saw Kelly and Troy waiting for her.

"Hi!" she chirped. "I remember you."

Troy looked puzzled. "You seem pretty cheery for someone whose friend just died."

Kelly looked at Troy. "I guess you heard about Paula."

"The police stopped by this morning to ask me and Jeremy some questions." His eyes shifted quickly from tree to tree, as if he was uneasy with the subject. "I guess you guys must have told them about us breaking in."

"Well, it did seem important," Kelly said.

"Yeah, I suppose in a case like this the cops have to look into every possibility." His glance refocused on Angel. "You're not upset about losing your friend?"

"Paula," Angel said thoughtfully.

"Yes?" Troy prompted when she didn't go on.

"Well, Paula and I weren't really friends. Of course I never wished evil on her. I'm surprised they let anyone hurt her."

Troy looked at Kelly. "I have no idea what she's talking about."

"Angel has a special way of thinking about life. When I heard someone following us in the woods, she told me it was my guardian angel."

Troy's eyes turned thoughtful for a moment before he grinned. "Cool—I guess."

"They *are* all around us," Angel stated as if this were a scientifically proven fact like, *gravity pulls things down to the Earth* or *eight ounces equals one cup*. She fixed Troy with a penetrating look. "Sometimes they become visible, you know. Sometimes they take the form of a person and help people who most need help. Are you Kelly's angel, Troy?"

Troy took a step back and choked on a laugh. "Man, you really are . . . different."

Kelly smiled. He had been about to call Angel something much less flattering, but had at the last second decided to be nice.

"Thank you." Angel fluttered her eyelashes at him as if he'd complimented her.

Kelly was getting much too cold to enjoy the weirdness of the conversation. "I'm freezing," she said. "If you want to talk some more, let's go inside the cabin."

They started walking again. Angel marched on ahead, but she kept turning around and grinning at Troy over her shoulder.

"I think she likes you," Kelly said, trying not to laugh when panic flashed through Troy's eyes. "Don't worry, she's harmless. Most of the time, I think she's just putting on an act to get attention."

"What about the rest of the time?" Troy whispered, after Angel turned again and beamed at him.

"I'm not sure," Kelly said, and she was only half teasing him. Angel had always been a mystery to her.

As soon as they were inside, Kelly realized how terribly wet and cold she was. The warmth of the fire, which leapt around the huge chunks of wood Will was hefting onto it, somehow made her feel all the more shivery.

"I've got to get out of these wet things," she said, glad it was the boys' room and not hers that was off limits. She unbuckled the fanny pack and hung it over her jacket then ran into the bedroom to change.

Closing the door, Kelly peeled off soggy jeans, socks, and sweater. Her ski jacket was fine for snow that could be brushed off immediately. But it wasn't totally waterproof. Even her underwear was soaked through.

Quickly, she towelled off, used a little baby powder to dry up the last few damp spots, and pulled on cozy sweatpants and a top. She stuck her feet in fuzzy slippers her dad had given her for Christmas. Sewn over the toes were white bunny heads with pink eyes and long, floppy ears.

When she stepped back into the den, Jeff and Nathan were back. Troy took one look at her feet and burst out laughing.

"What's with you?" she asked, sticking her nose in the air and striding across the room as if she were wearing a ballgown and tiara. She gracefully deposited herself on the rug in front of the fireplace.

Jeff smiled. "Must be the first time he's seen you in your famous bunny slippers." He turned to Troy. "They've been known to reduce grown men to giggles."

Kelly sniffed imperiously. "Well, *I* like them."

"I do too," Troy said. "In your sweats, with them on, you look like a little kid ready to get tucked into bed."

Nathan was taking a long time hanging up his

jacket. He kept fumbling with it, knocking the other coats off while trying to get his to stay on a peg. Finally, Will went over and helped him.

"Did you find out anything important?" Jeff asked.

"Paula took a Trailways bus from Baltimore to get here," Kelly said. "And she wasn't released from the hospital by her doctor. She sneaked out. No one knew she'd come here."

"Poor thing," Isabel murmured. "She was on the run. She probably hated it there, locked away like that."

"A whole year in that place," Chris said, shaking his head. "Man, that would drive me up a wall."

"Prison would have been a lot worse," Jeff reminded them. He turned to Kelly. "Is that all?"

"Yeah, what about you?"

"Nothing," Jeff said. "At least, nothing that will help you. A couple of kids staying in other cabins told us they'd thought someone had been in their stuff. But nothing was missing so they didn't report a break in."

"But that's *something*," Kelly said. "If there's been a thief working the area, and he surprised Paula—"

Jeff was already shaking his head. "If nothing was missing, there's been no robbery. Those guys probably just thought they'd put stuff in one place and forgot that they'd moved it."

"I think he's right," Troy said.

Kelly sighed. "What about anyone else?" She looked at Will, who was staring solemnly at his hands, in his lap.

"Zilch," he reported. "You know, I've been thinking. If I ever find out who did that to Paula . . ." His fists clenched and unclenched, as his eyes darkened past black.

The day Paula had died, she and Will had been

flirting, having fun. Had they been more than new friends?

Kelly couldn't imagine Will as the kind of boy who'd fall for any one girl that fast. But maybe she wasn't giving him enough credit for being sensitive. Paula might have been special to him.

"They'll get whoever's to blame," Kelly reassured him softly.

Will studied her for a moment. "I know it's not you, Kelly," he said. "I just want them to nail the guy."

"We all do," she said.

Troy left to rejoin his own group, but everyone from Thomaston High was at the cabin for lunch. Isabel said she had a craving for pizza. Pizza with *everything* on it.

It turned out she was serious about the everything part.

Kelly and Angel stood by, watching her pile sliced onions, mushrooms, green peppers, pepperoni, mountains of shredded mozzarella cheese, cooked sausage, ground beef, and pineapple on the tomato sauce—covered crust she'd prepared.

"I don't know how you can stay so thin when you eat like this," Kelly said. "I'd constantly stuff my face if I knew how to cook like you do."

Isabel shrugged. "I like to cook for other people more than for myself." She shot a concerned look at Kelly. "It wouldn't hurt you to have a couple of slices. What do you weigh now anyway?"

"I don't know." Kelly turned her back on her. She didn't want to talk about it. Other things were more important. "It doesn't matter."

"How's it coming?" Annette asked, bursting through the kitchen doors.

"It looks delicious," Kelly said, although her stomach spasmed at the smell of the spicy ingredients. She couldn't explain how she could be hungry but nauseous at the same time. The thought of putting all of those different foods in her stomach at the same time was revolting.

"How long before it's done?" Angel asked.

"Twenty minutes," Isabel said. "I think I'll make another one, just in case the boys decide to pig out. We should make sure there is *plenty* for everyone." She looked meaningfully at Kelly.

As if taking his cue from Isabel, Jeff stuck his head around the corner from the den. "Make extra. We've got company."

His eyes met Kelly's. "Your good buddies— Garrett County's finest—are back."

Kelly's stomach lurched and she gripped the edge of the counter.

Annette stepped over beside her. "There's no need to worry, Kelly. They're just doing their job. They probably stopped by to tell us who their latest suspect is—some drifter who's been seen in the area."

Kelly grimaced. "I hope so." But she wondered . . . How many serious crimes went unsolved every year in the United States? Hundreds . . . thousands?

Carrying the hollow feeling with her, she walked back into the den with the others. Isabel stayed behind to put the pizzas into the oven.

Will let Shellborn and Baxter in through the front door. Neither cop was smiling.

Shellborn walked straight over to Annette. "We received an anonymous telephone call about an hour ago, concerning one of your students," she said. "Did any of your group use a phone around that time?"

"Well . . . I don't know," Annette said, sounding confused. "Frank and I were here the whole time, and there's no telephone in this cabin. The kids came and went during the morning and early afternoon. I think some of them were out talking to residents of other cabins, trying to find out if they'd seen anything strange around here yesterday."

Frank wheeled himself out of his bedroom. "Back again, are you?"

"Yes, Mr. Riley," Shellborn drawled in her quiet way. She turned to Kelly. "Where were you about an hour ago, young lady?"

"I didn't make that phone call, if that's what you're thinking," Kelly said quickly.

"I don't suppose you did," the woman said. "I just want to know where y'all were."

"Walking around the woods, down to the lodge and back."

Annette was frowning at the police officer, as if wondering why she was singling out one of her students. Frank clamped his hands to the wheelchair arms and began pumping himself up and down.

"Were you with anyone, or alone?"

Tiny, prickling beads of sweat rose on Kelly's upper lip. She didn't know why she should react as if she were guilty of something when she hadn't done anything wrong.

"I was with Angel. Partway back, we ran into Troy."

Shellborn made a note on her clipboard, murmuring in her Atlanta accent as she wrote. "Angel and Troy . . ."

"What's this all about?" Kelly asked. "I haven't done anything wrong."

Shellborn avoided connecting with her eyes. She turned to Frank and Annette, who'd suddenly gotten very quiet. "About an hour ago, we got an anonymous phone call. The caller—we couldn't tell if it was a male or female—claimed to have seen Miss Peterson here enter this cabin around the time of Paula Schultz's death. She was then alleg-edly seen to leave it a short while later."

"But that's impossible!" Kelly cried. "I was skiing the whole time. I never came back here. Other kids were with me!"

"Not the entire time," the woman cop told her grimly. "You're an excellent skier, I'm told. It might take someone who's very fast ten minutes or less to ski down from the top of Wisp, cut through the woods, and back here to the cabin. You might have killed the girl, then continued skiing the rest of the way down to the lodge and met up with your friends again. No one would notice if you were out of sight for twenty minutes or so."

Suddenly Kelly couldn't breathe. The den seemed to revolve around her in a sickening swirl. Faces, flames, log walls . . . all swirling hopelessly. "I—No, that's impossible. It's a lie!"

"Of course, the call might have been a hoax," Shellborn admitted. "That's why we're here. We want to let all of you know that playing a joke like this on a friend is no laughing matter." Her steely gaze settled on Nathan, then shifted to the other boys in the room, as if guys might be more likely to play such a dangerous prank.

"If anyone called in that statement as a joke, you'd better tell us now," Baxter advised.

No one said anything.

Shellborn turned back to Kelly again. "You'd better come with us down to the station. We need to talk."

Kelly stared at the cop in disbelief. As worried as she'd been that they might blame her for Paula's death, she'd never foreseen this particular scene *really* happening.

"Are you *arresting* me?" she choked out.

"Just come along, miss," Baxter said. "We need to straighten some things out."

"Wait!" Frank shouted. "You can't drag one of these kids away without just cause. Do you have a warrant for the girl's arrest? You don't have proof she did anything wrong—just a phone call from some jerk with a warped sense of humor."

Annette flashed a surprised but grateful look at her husband. "He's right. Kelly Peterson is in my charge. Unless you can show some proof that she did anything wrong—"

"We're not arresting her," Shellborn said. "We just need to talk with her, and there's no place to do that here, in privacy." She waved Kelly toward the door. "Which is your coat? It's cold out."

Oh sure, Kelly thought wildly, *you're hunting for an excuse to send me to Death Row, but worried I'll catch the sniffles on the way.*

Her parka couldn't have dried out yet, but she didn't care. "The blue one," she murmured. "On that hook by the door."

Then all hell broke out.

Jeff rushed at Baxter, begging to be allowed to come along with Kelly. Isabel shrieked and ran for the kitchen at the smell of burning pizza. Chris grabbed Annette by the arm and demanded that she do something to save Kelly. Frank started bellowing something about lawyers and civil rights.

Shellborn ignored them all, and Baxter prodded Kelly toward the door.

Moving in a daze, Kelly allowed herself to be shifted toward the door. Baxter reached up to lift a couple of other coats off of Kelly's. Her fanny pack slipped from between them and fell to the floor.

The zipper must have been left open. Her wallet, a stick of Lipsaver with sunblock, her weekly lift pass, and a crumpled piece of paper spilled out onto the floor. Kelly reached down to retrieve the items.

Shellborn seized her wrist before she could touch

anything. "I'll get this stuff for you, hear? Y'all just put on that jacket."

As she picked up each thing, the woman carefully looked it over. She didn't open the wallet, though. Kelly wondered if that was one of the no-no's in police work. Maybe that would be crossing some sort of invisible legal line.

But when she came to the slip of paper, she carefully turned it over as her hand floated in slow motion toward the zippered pack.

Kelly could see that something was written on it. The police woman seemed to read it over several times before changing the direction of her hand and handing the note up to Baxter. Her eyes were muddied with hidden thoughts. *Dangerous thoughts,* Kelly thought, holding her breath.

Baxter looked at her and slowly bobbed his head.

"What is it?" Kelly asked. "I don't recognize that paper. What was it doing in my fanny pack?"

"That's another thing we'll be talking about," Shellborn said.

Nathan made a lightning fast move and whipped the note out of Baxter's fingers. "Hey!" the officer barked.

Nathan didn't pay any attention to him. He started reading out loud.

Dear Paula,

I didn't think I'd ever see you again. Too bad you showed up. After what you did to Brian, I can't believe you'd have the nerve to come back here. The problem is, since they did *n't punish you, I will have to.*

You deserve to die, and everyone knows it.

Your One-time Friend,
Kelly

The words dropped into the chill silence, like old pennies sinking to the bottom of a fountain.

Kelly found her voice first. "I-I didn't write that!" She looked around at the circle of solemn faces. "Honest, I didn't write that note!"

Jeff stepped up beside her. "Kelly wouldn't do something like this. She wouldn't kill someone. She wouldn't even threaten to do it—no matter how upset she was about Brian."

Shellborn moved herself firmly between Kelly and Jeff. "We'd like you to come with us to the station. There are a lot of questions that need answers."

"Please," Annette pleaded, "this isn't necessary. Jeff's right, Kelly couldn't hurt anyone!"

"I might have thought that, too," Shellborn said tightly, her drawl thickening and spilling out over the words. "But that was before this here letter turned up. Now we have evidence of Miss Peterson's *intention* to murder Miss Schultz."

Kelly opened her mouth to protest, but nothing came out.

Shellborn took her by the upper arm, steering her firmly through the door and down the steps toward a patrol car.

Kelly felt a hand pressing down on her head, another pushing her gently from behind. Then she was in the back seat of the patrol car, and she closed her eyes and bent forward and wept into the fleecy knees of her sweatpants.

11

The black-and-white police cruiser bumped off down the rutted dirt road connecting the cabins on Wisp Mountain. Kelly was aware that Shellborn had climbed into the back seat with her. Baxter must be driving, she thought.

I didn't do anything wrong! a voice inside of her wailed.

But no one believed her. Kelly felt filled with undeserved shame.

They had gone less than half a mile when Shellborn said, "Pull over here. We're out of sight of the cabin."

The car rolled to a rough stop, and Kelly looked up, more terrified than ever. What were they doing?

"You can't make me confess to something I didn't do!" she cried out, her words snipped off like pieces of ribbon cut with scissors. "You can't make me talk to you without a lawyer."

"You're right, sugar," Shellborn drawled in a tired voice. "Listen, stop crying. You're not under arrest. I just wanted your friends to think you were."

"Why would you want to—"

"I'll explain everything to y'all in a few minutes." She poked her partner in the back. "Go ahead, Larry."

Kelly glared at Shellborn as the car started forward again. She hadn't looked very closely at the woman before this moment, but now she did.

Officer Shellborn's hair was cut short, framing her face. It was reddish blond, a lighter, less vibrant shade than her own, and it clung in waves close to her head. Her eyes were a soft hazel, not the ordinary tan she'd thought, whereas Kelly's were green—jade green with little gold flecks in them. She wasn't a big or strong-looking woman. In fact, Kelly thought that if she exchanged her uniform for a stylish dress like Jeff's mother often wore, she might actually look pretty, for someone her age.

"All right," the cop said, as if she had been preparing to make this speech for a long time, "this is how things stand—"

"I want to call my father. I want a lawyer."

"If that's what you want to do, you can telephone your father as soon as we reach the station," the woman said. "I expect your chaperon is already on her way to a phone. But you won't need a lawyer, sugar, at least I don't think so."

"Why not?" Kelly demanded. Now that the cop was talking to her as if they were equals, she felt braver. And she wasn't sure she liked being called sugar.

"Like I said, we haven't arrested you. We're not charging you with murder. I want you to understand that. I just need for you to cooperate with us for a little while. Consider yourself under protective custody, as a possible witness."

"I didn't see Paula get killed."

"You're still involved in some way. Until I figure out how, I'm going to keep an eye on you, Kelly. That's pretty hard to do the way you ski."

Kelly looked at her hard. Was that a twinkle in her eye? "You've been following me?"

"No." But her answer came out on a measured

breath, as if there was more to it than a simple syllable. "I just know you can move pretty fast on those skis when you want to."

Kelly caught herself smiling at the compliment, then something occurred to her—she hadn't skied since Paula's death. If Shellborn had seen her coming down the mountain, it would have to have been before the murder. Kelly straightened out her lips. "I wish you hadn't taken me away from my friends that way."

"I wanted everyone to think we've found our chief suspect." The cop took a deep breath then wrinkled her nose, as if the gesture made thinking easier.

There was a cloud of freckles across its bridge, and the little brown dots seemed to jump around when she did that. The gesture didn't look very coplike.

"You see," she continued, "someone rang us up this morning with that tip about your entering the cabin at about the time Paula was killed. Of course we'd follow up on a lead like that. Especially since you and Paula were both involved in an accidental death not very long ago."

"I told you I never *wanted* to kill Paula. I wouldn't do that. Brian's death was behind us. We'd made up."

"I believe you. At any rate . . . we got that telephone call. Something about it wasn't right. The caller wouldn't identify him or herself. They just said you'd gone into the cabin then left again near the time Paula died. They didn't say when that was."

"The statement was very carefully worded," Baxter said from the front seat, "as if the person was afraid of saying too much or making a mistake."

"You couldn't recognize the voice?" Kelly asked.

"It's on tape. We record all incoming calls. I'll

play it for you. But the words were so muffled it would be difficult for anyone to identify the speaker."

"But the note," Kelly said. "I didn't write it."

"I realize that," Shellborn rubbed the inside corners of her eyes with one finger and thumb. "It wouldn't make sense if you had."

Kelly frowned.

"Think about it," Shellborn said as her partner pulled onto a wider road, "if someone writes a note threatening a person's life, they generally give the note or send it to that person. Either we'd find the note in the victim's possession, or, more likely, the killer would do everything he could to retrieve the note and destroy it."

"Then that proves I didn't write it."

"Not necessarily. But I have a feeling when we compare handwriting, there will be at least a subtle difference between yours and that in the note." Shellborn took the slip of paper off her clipboard and looked at it again, then put it back under the clamp. "Then there's this strange coincidence . . . Soon as we show the slightest suspicion of one person—you—we start getting tips over the phone and an incriminating note conveniently falls at our feet."

"It's like someone is trying to make your job easier for you," Kelly remarked.

"Exactly. And this job is never easy. Never."

Baxter chuckled. "You can say that again. Although we don't get a lot of murders out this way. It's usually something far less dramatic."

"So, what are you doing with me if you don't believe I'm the person who killed Paula?"

"With y'all's cooperation, we're going to play a mind game with the real killer."

Kelly laughed. "Do I have a choice?"

"Certainly, you do. We can drive you back to the

cabin and drop you off, explaining there was a problem with the evidence. Baxter and I can go back to the routine stuff—interviewing, looking for evidence we might have overlooked. It will be slow going, and meanwhile the trail will get cold. The first forty-eight hours of an investigation is crucial. After that, without a solid lead, we might never find Paula's killer."

Kelly shook her head. "That would be terrible."

"I have to warn you, though, there might be some danger involved."

"Because this person has already killed once?" Kelly asked.

"Exactly. And we don't believe this was a random act of violence."

Kelly's nerves prickled. "Then you've ruled out the possibility that Paula surprised a thief?"

"We don't think that's what happened," Baxter repeated from the front seat. He lit a cigarette with one hand while steering around a corner into the business section of town.

"You see," Shellborn explained, "there's been another investigation going on that might have something to do with Paula's murder."

"What kind of investigation?" Kelly asked.

The car stopped in front of a brick building. "Come on inside and I'll explain what I can," Shellborn said.

Kelly looked around the small duty room that held a half-dozen gray metal desks and assorted office equipment. The turkey sandwich she'd ordered sat on a piece of foil next to a diet soda. She picked up one half of the sandwich and took a nibble.

Baxter had gone off somewhere, but Shellborn sat on the other side of the desk, munching on potato chips and an Italian submarine sandwich.

"The thing is," Shellborn said, her eyes growing brighter the further she got into her story, "about a month ago, Baltimore County police requested help with a drug investigation. They were trying to trace supply lines of controlled substances into some of their public schools."

"You think Paula was killed over drugs?" Kelly asked. She couldn't imagine the connection, unless Paula had just stumbled on a deal.

"It's possible. I can't go into details now."

"So what do you want me to do?"

"First, I have to say that I might be wrong about my hunch that drugs have anything to do with why Paula died. In that case, you're not totally in the clear," Shellborn said solemnly. "We may turn up evidence that steers us back to you. But I'm inclined to believe you when you say you didn't kill that girl. The coroner's report states that the knife wound was really deep. It was caused by a forceful thrust. Someone very strong or enraged to the point of abnormal strength inflicted it."

"Like a guy?"

"Maybe. We don't want to rule anyone out yet." Shellborn took a bite of her sandwich and chewed. "Now, as to your job. I want to keep you here overnight, maybe part of tomorrow too. We'll move you around between the jail and the courthouse, but won't say anything too helpful to the press. You'll do a couple of perp walks—"

"Perp walks?" Kelly asked.

"Yeah, you see them on TV all the time. Some guy who's been arrested is escorted in handcuffs out of a building with a jacket thrown over his head. The police hustle him into a car and drive off. The cameras go crazy. Reporters make wild guesses about his guilt."

Kelly rolled her eyes. "My dad is really gonna like this."

"It'll be okay. We'll call him and let him know what's happening. He might want to stop answering his phone for a couple of days though."

Kelly shook her head. "You don't understand. My dad is really, really strict. He gets upset if I stay out after midnight on a weekend. He caught me drinking a beer at a friend's party, and he put me on restriction for two weeks. Two whole weeks, can you believe?"

"Good for him. He sounds like a father who's doing his job."

"I guess," Kelly said glumly, but she did love him a lot and she knew he cared about her.

"What about your mom?"

Kelly put down her sandwich and swallowed, even though there was nothing in her mouth. "She left us a long time ago."

Shellborn winced. "Sorry 'bout that, sugar. Well, it makes things simpler in a way."

"What do you mean?"

"Mothers tend to get hysterical about daughters involved in anything with the police." She laughed. "My mom thinks I'm crazy for wanting to be a cop."

"Really?" Kelly asked. "I think it's a great job for a woman."

Shellborn smiled, and her smile was all sunshine. Kelly understood why she didn't use it on the job. It made her look too sweet and cuddly.

"At any rate," the cop continued, reclaiming her official face, "we'll keep you busy just long enough to convince people we're considering you our only suspect. That should make the real killer less careful of his next moves."

"And you think that might involve delivering drugs to someone in Baltimore?"

"Maybe, or maybe he'll just clear out and move his operations somewhere else. The thing is, your arrest, real or not, should prompt some action. And we'll be watching for anything suspicious."

"What if you don't catch this person in a day or two? I mean, it could be weeks . . . months! Will you keep me in jail all that time?" Missing a week or two of school wouldn't be all that bad, she figured, but she imagined that jail might not be the most pleasant place to be.

"No, we can't legally do that, and I'm sure your father would object. But if we have to release you, there's someone already in place who can watch out for you, just to make sure you're all right."

Kelly smiled nervously. "I hope you find this creep fast."

"We do too. Now eat that sandwich. I bought it for you out of my pocket, and we're not throwing any of it away."

Kelly sighed and obeyed and chewed, although she didn't taste anything in her mouth. Still, her stomach seemed to feel a little better after a few bites.

"This person who you say is *in place* . . . Are you talking about another cop who's been watching us?" That would account for Shellborn's remark about her skiing.

"It's better if I don't say."

"But what if you let me out in two days, and you still haven't caught the murderer? What if someone comes after me and I need help?" She thought about the incident in the woods. Had it been Troy shadowing her, even though he'd denied it? Was there someone else in the woods with her and Angel? The cop assigned to the drug detail? Or had it only been her imagination? "I mean, what do I do if someone attacks me? I won't know who to go to, or how to call for help."

"For now, it's better you not know." Shellborn took a man-sized bit of sandwich and chewed energetically. "You might react differently to that person and, without meaning to, tip off the killer that there's an undercover cop on the prowl. That could jeopardize both of your lives. And it could blow both the drug case and the murder investigation."

"I see," Kelly said. But that didn't stop her from being curious. Would she recognize the person working for the police? Maybe it was one of the guys or girls on the ski patrol? Or someone in one of the neighboring cabins? Maybe even someone in the ski club?

She decided, no matter what Shellborn said, she'd better find out, just in case.

12

Jeff waited on the cabin porch for Annette to return from the lodge. She'd driven down to call Kelly's father. He hadn't wanted to stay inside with the other kids. All they were doing was talking about how shocked they were that Kelly had stabbed Paula.

He didn't believe it for a second.

Jeff paced the creaky wooden boards and blew frosty clouds between his lips and watched for the Rileys' Jeep. At last, it ground its way up the hill, through the soaring pine trees.

"We have to do something for Kelly," he said, intercepting Annette before she could step out of the car. "We can't just let the police drag her off then create a fake case around her. You know she didn't do it!"

She swung the door closed and started toward the cabin. Her face was taut, as if the skin had been stretched over the bones, almost to the point of breaking. "I don't know what to do," she said. "This is a nightmare."

"Is Mr. Peterson coming to Wisp?"

"Yes." She seemed reluctant to pronounce the word, as if it were painful say it out loud. "He was very upset. Very angry. I think he blames me for letting Kelly get into trouble."

Jeff felt badly for Annette. "He's a really nice man. He just loves Kelly a lot. He gets real protective of her. Took me a long time to get used to him, but we're okay now."

Annette didn't seem to be listening as she clomped up the steps.

"Can I take the Jeep into town?" Jeff asked impulsively. "I want to make sure Kelly's all right."

The teacher turned to face him on the porch and frowned. "I should go see her too, but the police said . . ." She took a deep breath, then appeared to collect her thoughts. "We'll wait for Mr. Peterson to arrive, which should be in less than four hours. I'll suggest the three of us go into town together."

Kelly sat in lock-up cell C where Officer Baxter had left her an hour earlier. It was a very small room with beige plaster walls and a cot pushed up against one of them. There were no windows.

A small stainless steel sink with a paper cup on its rim sat in one corner. Beside it crouched a metal toilet that was clean but gave her the creeps just to look at. If she had to use it, anyone looking in the metal grate in the door would see her. Kelly shivered at the thought and decided she'd try to hold it as long as possible. Maybe Shellborn would take her out of the cell long enough to use the public ladies' room off the duty room.

"Knock, knock," a voice sounded from the hallway.

"Come in," she muttered.

"Y'all having second thoughts about playing this role?" Shellborn asked as she stepped inside, carrying a pile of magazines and two boxes of jigsaw puzzles.

"Are you sure there isn't another way to catch Paula's killer?" Kelly asked.

"You come up with one, we'll give it a shot."

Kelly grimaced. "Well, I don't have one, so I

guess we have to stick with this. Did you call my father?"

"Yes." Shellborn put the magazines and games on the bed. "In fact, I caught him as he was dashing out the door, on his way here. Mrs. Riley got to him first."

Kelly felt her skin go clammy. "Oh no."

"He sounds okay," Shellborn reassured her. "He calmed right down as soon as I told him what was going on."

"He's going to kill me."

"Why? You didn't do anything."

"You don't know my father. He'll figure I must have done something to make you suspect me in the first place. He'll tell me I'm not careful enough about choosing my friends."

Shellborn smiled. "I have a feeling you've picked some very good friends. That boyfriend of yours looked awfully worried about you when we took you away."

"Jeff." Kelly closed her eyes tight. "He must think I'm terrible. He must think I'm a murderer."

"He's probably just confused and wondering what's going on."

"I can tell him, can't I?" Kelly asked. "I can tell him about acting like I'm guilty so that you can trap the real killer?"

"No," Shellborn said firmly. "You can't tell him or anyone else, except your father. And I've already filled him in. He's the only one who needs to know." She flashed one of her sweet, little girl grins. "I don't want him suing me for false arrest."

"Great . . . wonderful . . . fantastic," Kelly muttered. "The instant method to lose all of your friends—get arrested for murder."

Shellborn laughed, her eyes sparkling. She patted Kelly on the back. "Relax. After all of this is over, you'll be the hero."

"If I live that long," Kelly said.

"We'll look after you," Shellborn promised. "Nothing can happen."

But Frank Peterson expressed the same concerns in much more forceful terms when he arrived at the Garrett County Police Station a few hours later.

"I understand your need to apprehend this person," he said, his eyes fixed grimly on Officer Shellborn after she'd explained more of the investigation's details, "but you're putting my daughter's safety and emotional welfare at risk."

"Of course we can't proceed without your permission, Mr. Peterson," Shellborn said. "If you feel that strongly—"

"I absolutely feel that strongly!" he snapped. "She's a seventeen-year-old kid, and you're pitting her against a dangerous criminal."

Shellborn shook her head. "She'll be safely locked in a cell right here, one floor away from me. We expect to be able to pick up the person who's responsible for Paula Schultz's death within a few days. Then Kelly can be released. Until that time, she'll be safer here, with me."

"And what if that doesn't work? What if two days from now, or three or five or a week, you have no one? This maniac could discover my daughter has been working with the police to entrap him. He might try to kill her too!"

"We've considered that, and as I've explained to Kelly, a police officer will be watching her to make sure no harm comes to her."

Frank Peterson shook his head with finality, and she knew Shellborn had lost the battle. "No. I can't let you use her this way."

Kelly glanced sheepishly at Shellborn. The cop looked like a little kid who'd been given a present, then saw it snatched away by the neighborhood bully.

"Wait!" Kelly said, holding onto her father's arm when he stood up from the table where they'd been sitting. "I want to do this, Dad. I *want* to help find Paula's killer."

"You're not going to risk your life to—"

"I'm not risking anything. Not really," she said, although she wasn't sure that was absolutely true. "The police have everything under control, and it's important to me, Dad. It's really important."

Her father glared at Shellborn as she too rose from the table. "A criminal arrest. This could show up on her records, it could affect her going to college."

The police woman shook her head. "We never officially booked Kelly. And, I promise, I'll personally vouch for her safety."

"Please, Dad," Kelly pleaded. "Just go home and let me do this. Brian would have wanted me to help Paula."

The mention of Brian's name seemed to have more effect on him than anything else that had been said. He and Brian had been very close. He gave her a shadow of a smile.

"Yes, I guess he would have." Frank Peterson turned to the cop who stood in front of him. He hovered more than a foot over her, yet she didn't seem intimidated. "I'm not giving you my approval, Officer. But I won't stop Kelly from doing this because it means so much to her. You'd just better make sure you know what you're doing, because if she gets hurt in any way—"

"I'll treat her as if she were my own daughter," Shellborn reassured him. "I promise, she'll be fine. If you like, I'll call you three or four times a day to update you on what's been happening."

Kelly held her breath as her father and the lady

cop locked eyes in a kind of mind meld. They seemed to understand each other. Her father wouldn't hesitate to demand Shellborn's job if anything happened to her, and the cop was telling him she'd make sure that wouldn't be necessary.

"All right," Kelly said. "Let's get this perp walk thing over with."

It wouldn't have been so bad if Jeff and Annette hadn't been in the duty room when Kelly and her police escort passed through. While Shellborn had been trying to convince Frank Peterson to go along with the plan, Jeff and Annette had apparently been kept waiting there by the desk sergeant. Kelly could tell from the looks on their faces that they were terribly afraid for her.

"I'm all right," Kelly called out to them as Shellborn and Baxter led her quickly past them in handcuffs. "Everything will be fine."

"Wait!" Annette cried. "Mr. Peterson, I thought you said you were going to make them let Kelly go."

"It may take longer than I'd thought," he said stiffly, walking behind the two police officers.

Kelly could see he was still upset. He'd always worried enough about her for two parents. *Daddy,* she thought, *I love you for that.*

"A couple of reporters are already out there," one of the other cops in the room warned them.

"Duck if you don't want your face all over tomorrow's papers," Shellborn said, steering Kelly at a half-run through the tall wooden doors and onto the sidewalk.

Kelly started to turn away from the cameras, then thought about Brian and Paula. Wouldn't it be better if the real killer saw her face in the paper? Wouldn't he be all the more convinced of his safety if the papers showed a picture of someone looking guilty as hell?

Kelly remembered rehearsing for the last school musical she'd done. She was best at singing and dancing, but she'd had to act too.

Get into the soul of the character! she told herself.

Just before they reached the car, she lifted her head and glared directly into the nearest camera lens. Defiant, maybe a little cocky—that was her. *So you caught me! I don't care. I did it and I'm not sorry.*

Her expression said all that to the camera.

The two police officers deftly slipped her into the back seat of the patrol car and jumped in. As they drove off, Kelly looked out the back window to see her father talking to Annette and Jeff. She knew he wouldn't tell them about the plan. He'd promised her he wouldn't.

In another five minutes, he'd start driving east, heading for home.

Home, Kelly thought. *I wish I were home right now.*

But she didn't have long to feel sorry for herself. The car whizzed through small-town streets and stopped abruptly in front of a white country courthouse with pillars out front that almost dwarfed the tiny building. Shellborn and Baxter took her through several corridors busy with people, who stared at her, probably wondering what she'd done to get herself handcuffed to a cop.

You'll find out in tomorrow's paper, she thought grimly.

They stopped at a door marked *Judge E. L. Finch.* "The judge is away today," Shellborn explained. "His clerk said he wouldn't mind if we used his chambers for a short while."

After killing half an hour in the room lined with

bookshelves of huge leather-bound volumes, they started off again. By now, word had gotten out that the police had made an arrest in the Schultz murder case, the only murder that had taken place in the past three years in Garrett County. Instead of two photographers, there were now four, plus four reporters.

"Officer," one of them shouted, "can you give us a short statement?"

"No," Baxter said gruffly, elbowing his way through the little mob.

Someone wormed past Shellborn and shoved a microphone into Kelly's face. "Why did you kill that girl?"

"I didn't kill anyone!" Kelly blurted out automatically.

Shellborn nudged the reporter out of their way and pressed down on Kelly's head, popping her into the car again.

Flashbulbs went off. Video cameras whirred. Questions bombarded her.

Off they went again.

Kelly groaned. "I blew it. I'm so sorry! I said I didn't kill her. I can't believe I was so dumb."

"Everyone claims they're innocent," Baxter said.

"You did just fine. Don't worry about it." Shellborn looked down at the handcuffs. "I'm sorry about those. We'll get them off of you as soon as we get back to the station."

"It's okay," Kelly said. "I think I'm getting used to heavy-metal jewelry." She rattled the chain linking her to Shellborn, like a silver umbilical chord between baby and mother. "Some of my friends would love these."

Shellborn rolled her eyes and laughed.

For two days Kelly chilled out in cell C. Shellborn nagged her into eating at least half of every meal that was brought to her. Jeff came by each day, and Kelly longed to be able to tell him what was going on. But she'd promised she would keep their plan secret, so all she could do was repeat what she'd shouted at the reporter.

"I didn't kill Paula. I wouldn't do that to anyone."

Jeff looked as confused and hurt and angry as he had the day she'd been taken from the cabin. Sometimes a hopeless look pasted itself to his face, as if he couldn't make up his mind how to feel.

Annette came too, but she spent more time in the duty room at the end of the corridor. Kelly could hear her arguing with someone, either Shellborn or another person who might have been the lieutenant that Shellborn sometimes referred to. Kelly could have kissed Annette for sticking up for her.

Meanwhile, all Kelly could do was wait. She read magazines and put both of the puzzles together, then took them apart and put them together again. She asked for paper and pen and wrote silly-newsy letters to a friend who had moved to Denver and to her aunt in Maine. She wrote another one to Jeff, explaining everything she wasn't allowed to tell him. She gave the first two envelopes to Shellborn to mail for her, and kept the one for Jeff under her pillow. Someday soon, she hoped she'd be able to give it to him.

When the third morning dawned and the police still were no closer to finding Paula's killer, Kelly tore up Jeff's letter and dropped the shreds into the trash can. She couldn't chance the wrong person seeing it and realizing her arrest was a trick.

That morning, Shellborn herself brought in Kelly's breakfast tray.

"I guess it's guilt. I wanted to be able to tell you it was all over, we'd caught our murderer and you could go back to your friends."

"But you haven't and you can't," Kelly said, spreading butter on one of three pancakes on the plate before her. She knew Shellborn wouldn't leave until she'd watched her eat at least one.

She still had little appetite, but she had to admit she felt stronger. And the dizzy spells that came and went and had become an expected part of her life, left her.

"No, we haven't caught our killer. I'm sorry."

Kelly sighed and sipped from the glass of orange juice. "So, what happens now?"

"We keep on watching, waiting for the killer to make a move."

"Maybe he or she has left Wisp," Kelly said. "Maybe it was someone passing through, who won't come back this way ever again."

Shellborn studied the plate of pancakes as if it were a crime-scene clue. "You can eat one more. They're made without butter, you won't get fat eating them."

Kelly considered the plate. "Well, maybe a few more bites."

Shellborn looked satisfied. "I've thought of the stranger-passing-through theory," she said. "I hope it's not true, because then we may never solve the case." She looked solemnly at Kelly as she ate. "We have more reason than ever to believe the killer is still around. There's a lot at stake."

"You mean drug money?"

"Possibly, or something worth just as much." Shellborn looked around the tiny cell. "I've discussed things with my lieutenant. We're going to release you this morning. I'll make a statement to the press that we don't have enough evidence to continue holding you, but we still consider you a suspect."

"Won't releasing me make the killer a little nervous? I mean, he might think you're about to give up on me, that you're looking for someone else to blame."

"Maybe. It could still work to our advantage. He might try to plant more incriminating evidence to direct us back to you. Every time he manipulates the truth, he puts himself at risk. All we need is one good set of fingerprints, a hair, threads from clothing . . . there are dozens of ways to trace a person."

"What about my protection?" Kelly asked.

"Just as I promised, sugar, someone will be watching out for you," Shellborn said. "Now finish eating, and I'll call your chaperon to come for you."

13

Prickles, like a hundred tiny spider feet, scaled Kelly's spine as she followed Annette into the cabin. She didn't know what sort of reception to expect from the other kids. Even though Isabel was her best friend, only Jeff had come to see her at the police station. Did they all think she was guilty? That she'd killed Paula like the newspapers had said? She'd seen some of the articles; they sounded so convincing between their "alleged" this and "alleged" that.

When she walked in everyone was seated in the den, as if they'd been waiting for her.

Isabel glanced up from the couch at her then stared at a spot on the floor. Seated beside his girlfriend, Chris gave her a wary smile.

Kelly looked around and found Jeff. He sat cross-legged on the floor near Nathan and Will. His eyes met hers then. Like Isabel, he seemed at a loss for how he should act, and his glance fell away.

Kelly swallowed something lumpy and sour, and wished she could become invisible.

"Welcome back," Angel murmured, smiling from the doorway of the girls' bedroom.

"Ye-es," Isabel blurted out awkwardly, as if suddenly aware she'd slipped up on one of her duties as a best friend. "We're all glad you're back." But there were questions in her dark eyes, and her thin smile barely curved the corners of her lips.

Nathan seemed preoccupied with biting a hangnail off of one grimy finger. Will was making himself busy, poking up the fire to a roaring blaze. Reflections of the orange flames danced and flickered across his face.

Wheeling himself to the center of the room, Frank said, "It might be a good idea to clear the air a little, since there seems to be some tension about Kelly's coming back."

Annette's cheeks flushed bright pink. "I don't think that's necessary, Frank. It's not as if she's a convict returning to the community after twenty years in the slammer."

"I didn't say she was," he snapped. "What's the matter? Don't you think I can do *anything* anymore, just because I can't walk? Is that it? I can't even organize a meeting of your kids without your telling me how?"

Annette bit down on her bottom lip. "I didn't say that," she whispered hoarsely.

"You never say it, you just think it," he grumbled.

"I think it's a good idea," Kelly put in quickly. "I want to say something to everyone anyway."

She knew she couldn't tell them about Shellborn's plan, but the policewoman had agreed she could make a different sort of statement to her friends.

Kelly settled herself in the only vacant chair and took a deep breath. "I want you all to know that I didn't kill Paula. I guess the police thought there was enough reason to suspect me, but now they realize they don't have any real evidence."

Nathan snorted. "Oh yeah, what do they need these days? You standing over the body with a knife dripping blood?"

Jeff glared at him.

"Ignore him," Kelly said. She turned back to

129

Nathan. "The note that fell out of my pack and my friendship with Brian aren't enough. The note turned out to be in someone else's handwriting, and a lot of you were friends with Brian just like I was."

Will seemed to perk up. "I didn't know Brian. I wasn't even at Thomaston last year when he drowned."

"Do they have any idea who might have written the note?" Jeff asked.

"No," Kelly said honestly. "The police figure the person might have written with his left hand if he's right-handed to disguise his own writing, then used something I'd written to copy the shape of my letters. But it wasn't a very good job. They didn't even have to call in a handwriting expert to tell the difference."

"I saw on a TV show where this guy wrote one way when he was sober, and wrote in the handwriting of a totally different person when he was drunk or high on drugs," Chris said, looking pointedly at Nathan.

"Oh sure," Nathan snarled, "like I really care about your stupid detective game." He jerked around to face Annette. "When do we get out of this arctic paradise? I'm freezing my butt off and I need a drink—*like now!*"

"We'll leave as soon as the police say we can," she said tightly.

"Do you have anything more to say, Kelly?" Frank asked, slanting his wife a look that said, *like it or not, I'm still in on this.*

"Yes," she said. "The police told me they're totally convinced Paula didn't kill herself. They also believe the killer is still in this area. I just want to warn everyone to be real careful about going out alone."

Isabel shrank back against Chris's wide shoulder. He looked down protectively at her.

Nathan hummed nervously to himself.

Will threw another log on the fire. It landed with a loud crack, and everyone jumped.

"Did the police mention any suspects by name?" Jeff asked.

"No," Kelly said.

He nodded, and she could sense that each person in the room was absorbing the information, silently working out in his or her own mind the possibilities. A stranger? Someone on the ski patrol? A neighboring skier? Or someone in this very room?

Annette cleared her throat. "Well, as the girls have already said, we're glad you're back with us, Kelly. I'm sure everyone here agrees with me—," she looked pointedly at Nathan, "—that we never really believed you had anything to do with Paula's murder. In fact, I'm certain that even if Paula's killer is still around here, he's no one we know. I think a little trust is in order." She took a deep breath and let it out, done with her speech. "Now, how about some volunteers to help me start making lunch?"

Jeff pushed himself up off of the floor. Heading for the kitchen, he passed by Kelly's chair and touched her lightly on the shoulder. "I never thought anything bad about you," he said quietly.

"I know," she whispered, feeling warm inside all the same. It was reassuring to know Jeff hadn't believed the newspapers.

Jeff and Frank disappeared into the kitchen. Angel followed them. Will came over hesitantly and propped one blue-jeaned hip on the arm of Kelly's chair.

"Are you all right? I mean, they didn't hurt you or anything, did they?"

"No." Kelly giggled, relieved that the tension in the room seemed to have evaporated, like the puddles her boots had left when she'd come in from outside. "Did you think they'd beat me with rubber hoses or interrogate me all night under a spot light?"

He shrugged. "I didn't know what they'd do."

Kelly decided to change the subject to avoid having to explain what her days behind bars had really been like. "Have you guys been skiing much?" she asked.

"Some." She noticed a strain in his voice and wondered if he'd been thinking again of Paula. "No one's been really into it since . . . well, you know. I guess when someone you know dies, your heart isn't into skiing or much else."

What about Will's heart? She was sure, looking at the dark circles under his eyes, that his was broken. "You know, it's not your fault," Kelly said.

"Huh?"

"Just because you two were, well . . . getting pretty friendly, doesn't mean you should feel responsible for her."

Will squinted at her. "What are you talking about?"

"You and Paula. I saw you two kissing."

"Oh." He stared at his hands.

"You couldn't have protected her," Kelly continued. "You weren't even there."

Will shrugged, looking miserable. "I guess."

Solving the puzzle of Paula's death was, she thought, a little like playing with one of those letter-scramble games where you slide the little plastic squares around to spell out words or a design. Her dad put a different one in her Christmas stocking each year.

And now, a block of information seemed as if it had just fallen into place in Kelly's mind. The block that told her the identity of her guardian angel.

Of all the people in the cabin, only Will, Frank,

and Annette hadn't been at Deep Creek Lake when Brian died. Will and Annette had come to Thomaston High just that fall—Annette in September, at the beginning of the school year; Will in the middle of October. Shellborn had spoken of someone "already in place." Maybe that person was an undercover police officer who had been posing as a teacher or student while working on the drug investigation Shellborn had described. Annette didn't seem the type. She was too busy bickering with Frank. But what about Will?

Was he upset by Paula's death because he'd had a crush on her? Or was he angry with himself because, as an undercover cop, he should have been able to protect her?

Kelly looked up at Will, studying his smooth, handsome face and troubled eyes.

"What's wrong?" he asked.

"Nothing." She forced her gaze to shift away to the fire's flames. Shellborn had warned her not to try to contact the person shadowing her.

"There *is* something wrong," Will said. "I can tell. You're scared, aren't you? Why?"

"Why shouldn't I be? If the police are right, whoever killed Paula is still around."

"But why should that bother *you?* You haven't done anything to deserve getting killed for, have you?"

"No." That is, if you didn't count helping the police trap a killer. "But neither did Paula."

"You don't know that," Will said darkly. "None of us know what happened in that room." He jerked his head toward the taped-off bedroom door. "Listen, I *do* feel really bad about Paula. She seemed like a nice girl. I just want you to know, if anything scares you, or you just want to talk about things—anything at all—let me know. I'll be here for you."

Kelly studied his earnest blue eyes and nodded slowly. Was he telling her in a roundabout way that *he* was her secret protector?

In a strange way, it made sense. Will was the guy who, within a few weeks of enrolling at Thomaston, had gotten himself invited to three different parties, who managed to be in the bleachers at every football game, who wanted (or pretended to want) to be everyone's friend. Was he really only seventeen, like she was? Or was he a few years older? Just old enough to have gone through training for the Baltimore County police?

Kelly felt suddenly relieved. Will was in the cabin and he'd stick close to her when she went outside. No one would be able to hurt her.

"Thanks, Will," she murmured. "I appreciate it. Maybe I'll go help in the kitchen now."

"See you around," he said.

"Right."

They had an early lunch because half the kids hadn't eaten breakfast. Kelly ate almost none of the tuna sandwiches and tomato soup they made. Without Shellborn around to nudge food her way, she let her appetite determine whether she'd eat. She sipped at a small cup of the creamy orange-colored soup.

Kelly and Isabel washed up the dishes afterwards, then joined the other kids and Annette as they suited up to go out to ski. Only Frank planned to remain at the cabin.

The sun was shining, and the afternoon ski session had just started when they arrived at the lodge at the bottom of Wisp Mountain.

A crowd had already lined up for the lifts. The rains had melted away a lot of the earlier snowfall, but the massive snowmaking machines had been working overtime and four trails were open, thickly covered with manmade white stuff. The trails glittered in the noonday sunshine.

Kelly felt excited and hopeful for the first time in days. She wanted to ski, ski, *ski* until she was too exhausted to think about the terrible things that had happened.

"All right, let's gather round!" Annette waved them into a circle while they attached their lift tickets to their jacket zippers. "I've been watching all of you ski since we arrived at Wisp, and I've come up with a new list of qualifiers."

Kelly looked at Jeff. He seemed a little tense, and she wondered if he was nervous about his classification. Annette had cleared him to ski all of the intermediate slopes, but he hadn't been allowed to ski the advanced runs with her.

Although Jeff had been a good sport about it, Kelly knew it irritated him that she could ski black diamond trails and he couldn't. She supposed it was one of those guy things.

"Angel and Nathan, I want you two to keep to the slopes marked with the green squares. The beginner trails still have enough grade to be challenging for you. With a little more practice you'll be on the intermediates soon."

Nathan rolled his eyes. "Do I have to ski at all today? Isn't there something else I can do to kill time?" He looked toward the lodge.

"Skiing is good exercise," Annette said briskly. "You can't lie around the cabin all day."

"Try me," he grunted.

Either she ignored him or she didn't hear his comment. "Isabel and Chris, you may both move up to the intermediate slopes. Just don't take them too fast at first. You'll have to adjust to the steeper terrain. Remember to use a lot of wedge turns, especially if you get going too fast for good control."

Chris grinned. "Hey, practice pays off!"

Isabel smiled at him, then grinned triumphantly at Kelly.

"And Jeff, your technique has been looking quite strong these last few days," Annette said.

Kelly was surprised. Hadn't Will said no one had his heart in skiing? But Jeff had been pretty upset when she'd been arrested. Maybe he'd been burning off his frustration by working it out on the slopes.

"I think you're ready for a little more of a challenge," Annette continued. "You may try a black diamond trail today. But I'll accompany you on your first run."

"All right!" Jeff shouted. He turned to Kelly. "Now we can ski together more of the time."

"That's great," she agreed, equally pleased.

As they rode the chair lift to the top of Wisp, Kelly wondered if she should tell Jeff about Will. Then she realized she couldn't reveal Will's identity without breaking her promise to Shellborn.

Jeff chatted for a while about the slope and how he planned his run, but then grew quiet as they neared the top. She didn't have time to ask what he was thinking. The lift was quickly nearing the unloading zone.

Shifting her poles to her outside hand, Kelly lifted her ski tips, and edged forward on the bench seat. As the chair came up over the rise and started to swing around for its trip back down the mountain, she pushed off and glided with her skis in a wedge to the packed snow where other skiers stood adjusting their goggles and pointing poles off into the distance.

The view was gorgeous, the sky blue and clear, the air fresh and snappy—and she felt as if it had been three months instead of three days that she'd been locked away.

Kelly thought about cell C, and felt a cold flash of awareness of how awful it must be to spend years out of a lifetime in a place like that.

"You can't imagine how awful it was."

Jeff moved closer and put his arm around her. She realized she'd let her thoughts slip between her lips.

"Those cops don't know what they're doing," he said sympathetically.

"Maybe." Kelly ached to tell him everything. "Well, at least they figured out I wasn't the person they were after and let me go."

"I was really worried," he admitted.

She looked up at him and felt her heart go *ping,* the way it had the first time he'd kissed her. Jeff was so nice and so great-looking. She loved being held in his arms.

As if he were reading her mind, Jeff looped his poles around one wrist and reached around her to kiss her on the lips.

Kelly felt herself melting and wondered why all the snow around them hadn't turned into a puddle.

"Come on, quit smooching and let's ski, Mr. Black Diamond!" Annette shouted, laughing at them from a little ways off.

They started out as slowly as the mountain would let them. The trail dipped and charged over bumps, around clumps of trees and over short drops that could be avoided or taken as a jump. Annette crested each rise as easily as a snowbird.

Kelly skidded to a stop on the steep hillside to watch the teacher's form. "You can see what a great skier she must have been," she said into the wind when Jeff stopped near her.

"What do you mean? She still is."

"But she skied on an Olympic team!"

"She *almost* skied on an Olympic team," Jeff corrected her. "Remember, Frank got hurt at the qualifying meet and she dropped out of competition."

Kelly thought about the couple. "I don't understand them. She did that for him, and he treats her so awful."

Jeff nodded. "I know. It's weird. Maybe it's a pride thing. Like he can't admit to himself that she gave up an Olympic medal for him."

They pushed off, and Kelly had to concentrate on the mountain again. Devil's Drop was a difficult trail, even for her. She cut back and forth across the path, slicing against the snow, spraying it high into the air on her parallel turns, avoiding the rocks that sometimes poked up through a thin crust of ice left by the rains. This was one trail that was too treacherous for night skiing. They didn't even have lights along it, she noticed.

Halfway down, Kelly caught sight of a flash of brilliant blue. She looked to one side. It was a snowmobile, and it was speeding down the slope on the other side of a line of trees.

"He's going awful fast!" Kelly shouted at Jeff.

"Huh?" His eyes were fixed on the rugged trail ahead as he struggled to keep his balance and dropped behind her.

Kelly turned her head to see the snowmobile zip recklessly through an opening in the trees, then cut straight toward her.

She raised her arms above her head and waved them frantically. "Hey, watch out!"

But instead of steering out of her path, the machine veered closer. Panic rising in her throat, Kelly shifted her weight and leaned even further forward to try to force a turn and beat the driver to the line of trees on the right.

But it was no use. He was traveling much faster than she could on skis.

Kelly was aware of Jeff, behind her, shouting

something at the driver whose face was hidden behind a ski mask. Her heart pounded in her chest, and her mouth suddenly turned pasty dry.

She had a choice—continue straight down the hill and run into the side of the speeding vehicle, or ski to the left of it as it passed by. If she remembered this trail, to the left was a sharp drop of over twenty feet. She couldn't recall what was at the bottom. If it was rocks and trees, she probably wouldn't survive the landing.

But colliding with a snowmobile at full speed was as deadly as stepping off the curb into rush-hour traffic in downtown Baltimore.

She skied left—and was instantly airborne.

14

Kelly had never done any real jumping, at least not the kind she'd watched on TV during the winter Olympics when skiers soared for hundreds of feet off the end of a perilously steep ramp. But to ski a black diamond trail she had to know how to handle moguls—the irregular bumps and hollows patterning the snow. She'd learned to flex her knees and pop up over the high spots, taking to the air for a second or two before coming down on flexed legs and preparing for the next liftoff.

This was different. After a second . . . two seconds . . . three seconds, she was still flying. The wind rushed at her, swallowing her up like a huge whale, in one gulp.

She tried to remember what she'd seen Annette do moments earlier. Leaning forward, she kept her body rigid and in line with her skis. She held her arms out to her sides for balance. As she sliced down, down, down through the air, she tried not to look at her feet but fix on a point at the foot of the mountain. If she lost control now, she knew the fall might well kill her.

Just before her skis touched ground, Kelly glanced down to gauge the surface, flexed her knees, and took the shock of landing as if she had springs for legs. The skis bit into granular crystals, and she wedge-turned just short of a massive tree trunk.

Gasping for breath, Kelly threw off her snow-sprayed goggles and stared around her. Along the lip of the cliff above, she could see the snowmobile speeding away.

"You idiot!" she screamed, although it was unlikely the driver would hear her.

Annette reached her only a few seconds before Jeff. They'd both come around the long way.

"Are you all right, Kelly?" she asked, her face white with shock. Her hair was blown out from her face in every direction, and somewhere in her rush to reach Kelly she'd lost her knitted headband.

"I'm fine." Kelly swallowed, took a raspy breath, then swallowed again.

"That lunatic might have gotten you killed!" Annette shouted. "That's how skiing accidents happen—sheer reckless behavior. I'm going to report this to the ski patrol. Whoever he is, he shouldn't be allowed on the trails."

Jeff looked off in the direction the snowmobile had taken. "That was no accident," he said.

Kelly stared at him.

"Why would you say that?" Annette asked.

"I saw him look right at Kelly, then change directions to block out her only safe line down the mountain."

Kelly caught one word. "Him?"

"It sure looked like a guy to me," Jeff said.

Annette shook her head. "We shouldn't assume anything. In a bulky ski parka, with a full ski mask—that could have been a girl as easily as a boy. Or an adult my age."

Kelly nodded. Unfortunately, Annette was probably right. "Did you get the vehicle number on the skimobile?"

Annette let out a groan of exasperation. "No. What about you, Jeff?"

He shook his head. "It all happened so fast."

"I'll report the incident anyway," Annette decided, her eyes sparking with anger. "They should be more careful who they rent those things to."

Inside the lodge, Kelly and Jeff headed straight for the snack bar while Annette went in search of the ski patrol office. Kelly's throat felt as parched as beach sand at low tide. She bought herself a king-size paper cup of root beer. Jeff got in the food line. Like most boys, she thought, he never stopped eating.

While she waited for him, she went to look for a table and found an empty one near the windows overlooking the beginner slope and lift area. She watched the chairs on the #2 lift come down empty, make their loop around the pole that supported the cables, and start back up the mountain, many of the chairs occupied by skiers laughing, waving at friends, and trying to pull the safety bar down—all at the same time. Off to one side were the handle tow and rope tow that a lot of the beginners took to get to the top of the short run called Belly Flop.

She remembered learning to ski on that trail. Her dad had brought her and Brian up for a weekend when they were ten years old. She hadn't thought about that day in a long time, and it made her throat ache she felt so suddenly sad.

"Sure miss you, Bri," she murmured into her soda, then took a long, long drink.

"Hi there," a voice squeaked in her ear.

Kelly jumped, then let out her breath in a relieved puff. "Hi, Jeremy. I haven't seen you in a while."

"Haven't seen you either," another voice chimed in. It was Troy, carrying a tray with drinks and a plastic bowl of nachos piled high with gooey orange cheese.

"I've been sort of busy," Kelly said.

"So I heard. Decided to cool your heels as a guest of the Garrett County police while you waited for the rain to go away?"

"It wasn't my idea of a fun time, believe me," she ground out.

Jeremy looked surprised. "I didn't know they put girls in jail."

Troy laughed and thumped his friend on the back. "What do you expect them to do with some girl who knocks off her boyfriend or robs a fast-food store?"

Jeremy shrugged. "I just never thought of girls being . . . being violent," Jeremy said, smiling shyly at Kelly.

"Most of us aren't. Although I might change my mind the way things are going." Kelly told them about her narrow miss on the mountain.

"That's pretty wild," Troy agreed. He looked distractedly at the tray. "Hey, I forgot napkins, be right back."

Kelly eyed the nachos. They actually looked pretty good, but she was a little ticked off at Troy. The least he could have done was act surprised when she told him about her close call.

"Go ahead, help yourself," Jeremy said, after she'd stared at the nachos for a full minute.

Kelly picked up a chip drizzled with warm cheese and popped it into her mouth. "Which trail were you guys skiing?" Kelly asked.

"Oh, we weren't really skiing," Jeremy said.

She looked suspiciously at his wind-reddened cheeks. "You weren't?"

"Naw. I was taking a lesson at the beginner area. Troy thought it might be a good idea."

"Oh." Kelly helped herself to another chip.

Why was it ever since she'd been around Officer Shellborn she found herself eating again? Actually, she had to admit she was feeling different—better

143

in a way she couldn't really describe. Which was ridiculous because at the same time she was terrified that whoever had killed Paula would come after her.

A thought crossed her mind that had rattled around in it a few minutes earlier. Had that snowmobile rider been just a foolhardy kid? Or had he, as Jeff believed, intentionally tried to hurt her?

She looked across the crowded cafeteria, wishing Jeff would hurry back so she could talk to him. Maybe she should call Shellborn and tell her what had happened.

At last, she spotted Jeff. He and Troy had run into each other and were talking. "What was Troy doing while you took your lesson?" she asked, trying to make polite conversation.

Jeremy crunched on the chips noisily enough for a whole football team. "He said he was going to ski on his own for a while, but I saw him over at the snowmobile rental shop."

A warning tingle started working its way up from Kelly's toes. She grabbed for the nearest soda and sucked hard on the straw.

"Hey, that's Troy's drink!" Jeremy squeaked. "He might not like—"

She quickly exchanged cups. "When did you two meet up again?" she asked.

"Oh, my lesson ended just a few minutes ago. He was waiting for me in front of the ski school sign, right before we came in here."

Kelly spun around on the wooden bench. Troy and Jeff were heading across the room toward them. Jeff carried a tray with another order of nachos and a drink for himself.

Kelly shot to her feet and stepped in front of him before he could put the tray down on the table. "Let's take our stuff over there," she said quickly. "Bye, Troy . . . Jeremy. See you guys later."

She was aware of Troy frowning at her, his eyebrows thickening then lowering by inches as she grabbed Jeff's arm and shoved him off into a far corner of the snack bar.

"What's the matter with you?" he demanded. "I thought you *wanted* me to be friendly with Troy."

"I do . . . I mean, I did." She felt so confused. "I just found out something terrible."

"What?"

"Troy may have been driving that snowmobile."

Jeff stared at her. "What makes you think that?"

"Jeremy told me that Troy said he was going to ski. But he lied. As soon as he thought his friend was busy taking a class, he zipped on over to the snowmobile rental office. And Jeremy didn't see him again until just a few minutes ago."

"That's strange," Jeff admitted, sitting down on the bench along one side of the picnic-style table. "Maybe it's just a coincidence?"

"It's an awful big coincidence, if it is one," Kelly said. "I mean, he must have rented a snowmobile right about the time we were taking the lift to the top, but he kept it less than an hour. Why would he return it so fast?"

"I don't know," Jeff said. He glared across the room at Troy and Jeremy.

Kelly saw Troy glance their way, then quickly look out the window.

"What do you think I should do? Should I call Officer Shellborn?" she asked.

"Yeah, I guess you'd better."

Kelly found the phone booth she'd tried to use the other day, and this time it was free. She yanked open the hinged door and stepped inside. Hastily, she lifted the receiver while fishing for Shellborn's card in her purse.

Her hand was shaking so hard, she had to try

145

three times to get the number right. The phone rang once . . . twice . . .

A shadow fell across her as if someone had stepped between her and the windows overlooking Wisp. Before she could turn around, the booth's door opened and someone squeezed inside with her.

"Hey, what do you think—"

"Shut up!" a voice shouted.

A hand flashed in front of her face and pressed down the receiver lever, cutting off the ring. It sounded like a strangled seagull, caught mid-squawk.

"Wh-what did you do that for?" she demanded, wrenching herself around in the tight space.

Troy stared solemnly down at her. "You don't have to call anyone."

An ice-water chill dribbled down through each vertebra in her spine. "Why not?" she breathed.

He took the receiver out of her hand and replaced it in its cradle. "It's not necessary."

"If I don't call my dad every day, he worries about me." It was the first lie that popped into her head. She prayed it would be good enough as she palmed Shellborn's card, hoping Troy hadn't seen it.

"You're not calling your father, you're calling the police," he ground out.

"How would you know who I was calling?"

"I know, Kelly," he said. His tan eyes had lost their friendly sparkle and darkened nearly to black. "You didn't have to tell me what happened up there on Devil's Drop. I saw it."

After all the plays she'd performed in, she couldn't make herself act this time. "*You* were driving that snowmobile," she choked out. "You tried to kill me."

"No."

"You did. Jeremy saw you renting a snowmobile and—"

"I was only checking to find out who had signed them out that morning. I didn't rent one. I wish I had, it would have made it a heck of a lot easier for me to keep up with you."

"Why would you want to keep up with me if you weren't planning on killing me?" she demanded, her voice shaking as much as her hands.

Troy's back was pressed up against the booth's door. She couldn't figure out a way to get past him.

Troy looked blankly at her. "Think," he said.

Kelly felt as if her knees were going to give out on her any second. Her stomach twisted and heaved. "I think I'm going to be sick," she cried, gulping down the stuffy air in the booth.

"No, you're not," Troy insisted. "Now, *think!*"

Kelly stared up into Troy's face, just inches from hers. She'd never seen him from this close. He still wasn't a really handsome boy, not like Will, or even like Jeff. But now he seemed different from the other boys in a more important way. There was something shrewd and experienced in the way he was looking at her now. He seemed older without his smile. He seemed dangerous, or at least accustomed to danger.

"Sometimes," he whispered, "things aren't what they appear—that goes for people too."

Kelly drew a sharp breath.

"You!" Kelly gasped. "You're a cop!"

"Sh-sh," he said.

"You are, aren't you?"

"I told Shellborn and Baxter they should tell you or it would make things difficult. They didn't believe you'd be able to act normal around me without blowing my cover."

"So why are you telling me now?" she demanded, still suspicious.

"I don't want you trusting the wrong person. Besides, if what I've heard from the kids in your group is true, you're a talented enough actress to handle any role."

"So?" She tried to cross her arms over her chest, but there wasn't room.

"All you have to do is *act* as if you think of me as no different than the other kids," Troy said.

"I'm not sure I can trust you," she said. "I thought my watchdog was someone else."

"Who?"

"Will. He's pretty new at my school. I figured it couldn't be someone I'd known a long time."

"Will was the one who was flirting with Paula the day she arrived?" he asked, as if trying to sort out a detail that had confused him.

"Right."

He considered this for a minute. "Okay, you need proof," he said abruptly.

He took out his wallet and flipped it open to reveal a Maryland driver's license—the kind everyone in high school had with a photo in profile to show you weren't twenty-one, so you couldn't get served at a bar. There were also two movie-rental cards and a membership ID for 10% off all CD's at Planet Music.

"So?" Kelly asked again. She could be looking at any high school student's wallet.

Troy flipped the leather fold one more time to reveal a silver-colored badge. *Baltimore County Police,* it said above an embossed crest.

"That doesn't mean anything," she said. "Anyone can order a fake badge through the mail."

"You're making this hard," he grumbled. "Okay, call this number—," he leaned close to her ear, and his breath felt hot against her neck and earlobe, "—555-0174."

"Who am I calling?"

"You'll see."

She punched in the seven numbers. While the phone at the other end rang, she asked, "What about the driver's license?"

"What about it?"

"If you're under twenty-one, how can you be a cop?"

"It's a fake license."

In spite of her nervousness, Kelly giggled. "That's the first time I've ever heard of someone wanting a forged *under*-age license."

"I'm undercover—what do you want?"

A man answered the phone. "Baltimore County Police, Wilkens District, how may I direct your call?"

Troy hissed in her ear. "Ask for Officer Chase."

She did.

"He's out on a case, miss," the man informed her. "Can someone else help you?"

Troy was buzzing urgently in her ear again. "Tell him it's an emergency. Leave your number and ask him to contact Chase on his pager."

Kelly shoved him away by a few inches but did as he said, then she hung up. "Now what?"

"We wait," he said, and they stood there looking at each other until she felt as if she couldn't breathe because the air in the booth had been used up.

A second later, a high-pitched beep sounded from inside the phone booth. Troy plucked a small black pager from his pocket and flicked it off.

"See?"

"You're Officer Chase?" She squinted at him. "You could have the cop's pager. You could have stolen it, or killed him for it."

Troy made a face at her. "Let me at the phone."

After he'd punched in the same numbers he'd

given her before, he signalled her to press her ear close to the receiver. "Sergeant Tully, do you recognize my voice?" he said into the receiver.

"Hey there, Troy—knock off the foolin' around. You're tyin' up an official line."

"Sorry, but this is a kind of emergency. Tell me who I am."

"Troy—"

"Say it. I'm not screwin' around here. I need you to ID me for someone."

The sergeant let out a windstorm of a sigh. "You are Troy Chase—Chase to most of us. Are you still workin' under cover detail in those schools?"

"Right. See ya."

He hung up and looked at Kelly. "Convinced?"

"I guess I believe you," she said meekly. "Now tell me what's going on."

"Well, we're not sure yet." He cleared his throat and contemplated his next words. "See, I've only been with Baltimore County for about six months, and all of that time I've been assigned to a drug detail. We're trying to crack down on stuff being sold in the schools."

"You've been posing as a student," she guessed.

"Right. Because I look about seventeen, even though I'll be twenty-two this summer, they picked me to go undercover."

"What do you do?" she asked.

"Mostly, I just keep my eyes and ears open. I hitched up with Jeremy right away. Poor guy was desperate for a friend. He doesn't fit in with any real crowd at school, so he's sort of neutral— equally picked on by everybody."

"He doesn't seem like a very good way to meet a lot of kids," she commented.

"He's no social butterfly, but he knows everyone in the school by sight and name. He's a lot sharper than he looks. It wasn't long before he was telling me who in the school did drugs, where and when they bought their stuff, and who from."

"Then you arrested these people?" she asked.

"No. That's just it, we didn't want to throw a few amateur dealers in jail. We didn't want to arrest the high school kids and let the pros who were bringing crack cocaine and other drugs into the area remain free. So I laid low, kept on watching and added more and bigger names to the list."

Kelly frowned. "How did you end up out here? Is there a drug connection at Wisp?"

"We don't know. A bunch of kids from the school I'd enrolled in were coming out here for a ski club trip. Our detail has been watching the clubs, since some of the members are known users. There's also a chance that over spring break there might be a pick-up outside of the city for delivery when school starts up again. My boss figured a chartered bus would be a low-risk way to bring a shipment back into the city."

Kelly smiled, at last understanding one thing. "That's why you and Jeremy broke into our cabin. You weren't looking for his goggles. You were searching for drugs."

"Yeah, although Jeremy still thinks we were hunting for his goggles." Troy chuckled, shaking his head. "I hid them on him."

"Did you find anything?" Kelly asked.

"A couple of packs of cigarettes and a couple of Jim Beam miniatures in Nathan's suitcase. That's all. From what the other kids in your group have said about him, he's got some heavy problems."

Kelly nodded. "Poor Nathan, his dad's an alcoholic, and I don't know what happened to his mom. He takes every chance to get away from home for a while. He was straight for a while, when he was dating Angel. I think even she has given up on him." Kelly hesitated. "You think Nathan is dealing drugs?"

"No. My information says the kid never has any money. Whatever he earns at part-time jobs, he blows on cigs and booze. If he were dealing, he'd get his habit fed for free and be driving a Porsche."

Kelly shook her head. "He's not driving anything that I know of."

"Tell me about the others in your group."

"Maybe we should go somewhere else and talk," she suggested. "It's getting stuffy in here."

"But it's much safer. No one can hear us."

She supposed he was right. "Well," she continued, "you know Angel—she's a little confused about life, but other than that she's harmless."

"I remember you saying that. I wonder . . ." He looked at her for a moment then said, "Go on."

"And there's Jeff, my boyfriend, but he's the ultimate straight guy. He'd never do or sell drugs of any kind. He's very serious about that sort of thing."

"What about your chaperons?"

"Annette and Frank Riley? Annette is as sweet as can be. I love her, she's the best teacher and—"

"I wasn't asking for a recommendation for teacher of the year. Tell me what you know about her personal background. Have you ever heard her and her husband arguing about money? While they've been up at Wisp, have they left you and the others for long periods of time? Do you find kids with bad reps hanging around her in school—like for short tutoring sessions?"

Kelly laughed. "Oh yeah, I can see Annette, Queen of Exercise and Healthful Living, handing out samples of cocaine to her students."

"So eliminate her, what about her husband?"

Kelly's smile wavered. "He's different."

"In what way?"

"Well, it's hard to say. He and Annette fight a lot, and it's usually about nothing or at least nothing I can figure out."

"You've never heard their words?"

"Not many. I think it mostly has to do with his accident. See, they were both trying out for the Olympics. Frank was a jumper, and Annette was a downhill racer. In the qualifying rounds, Frank took a terrible fall. I heard Annette say once that it might not have been so bad, but his bindings didn't release the way they should have, and he landed all twisted up and injured his spine. He's paralyzed from the waist down, has to use a wheelchair to get around."

"He's a big man," Troy commented.

"Big?" Kelly considered this. Because she'd never seen Frank standing up, she hadn't thought much about his height or size. "I guess he's sort of strong. Annette says he works out with weights to keep his upper body in shape. But workouts don't seem to help his temper, like they do some people. He shouts at Annette all the time."

"Could they be arguing about something other than his injury? That seems a long time ago."

"Maybe." But Frank dealing drugs to students? It seemed too fantastic to believe. *Drugs,* she thought, *who else do I know whose life is tangled up in that word?* Kelly shifted mental gears. "Chris used to be addicted to anabolic steroids, to bulk him up for football."

"Sometimes using one drug will lead to others," Troy commented.

"I don't think so with Chris. His girlfriend Isabel helped him get off the steroids, and I'm sure he isn't doing anything else."

"What about her?"

"Izzy? She's the nicest girl. Her family is part

Navaho, and she's very into nature and conservation. I can't imagine her getting involved in anything illegal or violent."

"You have another guy in your group, don't you?"

"Will. He's very popular."

Troy's eyes brightened. "A promising sign. How well do you know him?"

"Not real well, he's only been at Thomaston since the beginning of this year. But I'm sure he doesn't do drugs. It's pretty obvious, the kids who are into that sort of thing."

"What *is* his thing?"

"Partying. He just likes being around people. He's a nice guy." She hesitated. "Well, he flirts a lot. But if a girl doesn't take him seriously, she can have a good time and won't get her feelings hurt."

Troy leaned closer to her, his eyes intense, drilling into her as if he could see through her body into her soul. "You've been to some of those parties."

She looked away from him, suddenly uncomfortable again. "Sure."

"At those parties, did he ever disappear for a while? Maybe go off with a few kids at a time then come back?"

"You're thinking he's dealing drugs at parties?" She laughed. "No, he's not like that at all. He arrives right on time and mixes for a while with everyone, picks up whichever girl he's been flirting with, and they leave early. He doesn't usually come back that night."

Troy grinned. "Quite a playboy."

Kelly shrugged. "As far as I know, the only crime Will's been involved in is breaking a lot of girls' hearts. But I don't think he means to hurt anyone. It's just the way Will is. He's crazy about girls."

Troy looked a lot less happy. "We're running out

of possibilities, unless you're wrong about one of your friends."

Kelly swallowed, hoping she wasn't wrong. "It's still possible that a stranger—someone I don't know, who isn't even involved with the drug dealers you're trying to catch—killed Paula. Right?"

"Anything is possible," he admitted.

"So you still have a lot of looking to do."

Troy nodded. "Everything we've gotten so far indicates something important is about to come down. Maybe it's a really big shipment. Maybe there's been some kind of shake-up in their distribution system—who knows. But, so far, we haven't been able to put together enough information to make sense of it." Troy shook his head, looking disappointed. "Listen, you'd better get back to your boyfriend before he comes looking for you." He shoved open the door of the booth and backed out, letting in a puff of fresh air.

"How do I get hold of you if I need you?" Kelly asked.

Troy picked up a Wisp Special Events schedule from a stack of brochures in a rack near the window. He wrote two phone numbers on the inside flap of one and handed it to her.

"The first one's the Garrett County police station, local—the same one you'd call to get Shellborn. The other is my cabin. We made sure to get one that had a phone in it." He winked at her. "Who says cops are dumb? Anyway, chances are you won't need either one. I'll be within shouting distance most of the time. Maggie asked me to stay close by."

"Maggie?" she asked, confused.

"Officer Margaret Shellborn. Maggie," he said. "At any rate if I'm not around and you get scared, just pick up a telephone and call."

Kelly looked at the numbers. Would having them really help? How much time did Paula have before the killer stabbed her through the heart?

Not enough time to find a telephone, the answer came to her.

15

Jeff waited for Kelly in the snack bar. She'd been so upset by that jerk on the snowmobile, and he couldn't blame her. But had it really been Troy driving it? He didn't particularly like the guy, but accusing him of murder was stretching things a little. Still, it did seem strange that Troy had lied to his friend then been seen at the snowmobile rental office just before Kelly's run-in with the speeding vehicle.

Jeff looked up from the chunks of ice in his soda to see Troy walking away from Jeremy. He quickly looked away, so that it wouldn't appear he was watching. But he could see Troy's reflection in the window overlooking the slopes. Jeff watched him glance around the room once, as if to make sure no one was looking, then he ducked down the hallway Kelly had taken a few minutes earlier.

Jeff sat rigidly on the wooden bench, waiting, but Kelly didn't come back. He started to worry. What if she hadn't been able to reach the police? What if Troy had caught her making the call? Would he hurt her?

Jumping up from the table, Jeff ran across the snack bar and followed the blue-and-white signs to the public phones at the end of a corridor. But he stopped short, then hastily stepped back around the corner when he found her.

Troy stood with Kelly in an old-fashioned telephone booth, his arm braced over her shoulder and against the inside wall. Their heads were pressed cozily together as they talked. Kelly hadn't even bothered to pick up the receiver to make it look like she was making a call. She didn't look at all afraid of Troy. In fact, she was smiling.

A slow sourness crept into his stomach. Jeff charged forward two steps, then stopped himself as the anger boiling up inside of him shrank to a small, burning coal in his chest. Kelly had lied to him.

The realization hit him so hard, he staggered backward another step. Why had she made up the story about Troy? Was it just an excuse to make a phone call to the cops—one she evidently hadn't bothered making? Was it all so she could meet Troy at the booth? And then what? *Maybe she's trying to work up her courage to break up with me,* he thought. It would be like her to not want to hurt his feelings. Maybe she just didn't know how to tell him she liked Troy more than she liked him.

Jeff spun around and loped off down the corridor before either Kelly or Troy could see him. Back at the table, he threw himself onto the bench and seized the paper cup of soda. He took a sip, but the liquid tasted flat, with no flavor. It might as well have been water.

Mechanically, his hand moved toward the bowl of cold nacho chips, the ones he'd saved for Kelly. The cheese was rubbery and lay on his tongue like a coating of plastic.

When another five minutes had passed and Kelly still hadn't come back, Jeff pushed himself up from the table and walked outside. He had to get some cold air into his lungs to start his brain working again. He had to decide what to do—break up with Kelly or smash Troy's face. Maybe he'd do both.

It was almost ten minutes later when Kelly ran

out through the doors of the lodge, squinting into the sunlight that reflected off the new machine-made snow. Her red hair gleamed, and her face was flushed. He didn't want to think why.

Jeff stood beside the ski and boot racks, waiting for her to spot him.

At last she gave an excited little jump and waved. "I've been looking all over for you!" she cried.

"Really," he mumbled. He wished he didn't feel like this—as if he'd swallowed a mouthful of gravel and it was resting heavily in his stomach. He wished he could think of something cool to say, something to make him feel as if he'd been the one to decide they should go different ways . . . for his own reasons.

Kelly blinked at him, as if she suspected something was wrong. "I thought you'd gotten tired of waiting for me and had gone up the mountain without me."

"I was considering it."

"Do you want to ski some more?"

He could tell she was puzzled. *Tough,* he thought, *if you can't be honest with me, there's no reason I should be straight with you.*

"I'm going to ski, but I'm going up alone," he said at last.

When Jeff started to step around her, Kelly moved in front of him. "What's happened?" she asked. "Everything was fine when I left you at the table."

Jeff rolled his eyes. "That was before you lied to me. You said you were going to call the police. But you sneaked off to meet with your new boyfriend."

"Boyfriend?" Suddenly the color in her cheeks leaked away. "You saw me at the phone booth?"

"Yeah." His stomach ached. He pictured her squeezed up against the glass wall, Troy embracing her.

"Jeff, you really don't understand."

"He had his arm around you."

"He did not! We were just standing sort of close. It's not like *that* at all."

"So what's it like?" he spat. "Are you going to tell me he's just a friend like Chris is or like Brian was? You only met him a few days ago."

"I-I know," Kelly stammered. He could tell she was thinking hard, her eyes flickered from him to the mountainside and back again, as if searching for an answer that would satisfy him.

"If you want to break up, just say so," Jeff muttered.

"No!" she shouted. "That's not what I want."

Jeff shook his head. "I don't believe you, Kelly. This is the third time this has happened. If you and Troy don't have something going, then tell me why you two were huddled up in that phone booth together when you said you were calling to report him to the cops."

Kelly gazed up at him, her green eyes swimming in pools of tears. "I-I can't—"

Jeff nodded. "Fine. No hard feelings then. I'll see you around."

He turned and started to walk away, still thinking she'd run to stop him and promise she wouldn't see Troy anymore. But she didn't. And he kept on walking. And his heart crumbled a little more with every step he took.

Kelly didn't know what to do. She watched Jeff plod away across the packed snow at the foot of Wisp. His shoulders were hunched, his head low, his dark hair falling over his forehead.

She ached to tell him everything Troy had told her, but she knew she couldn't if she wanted to help catch Paula's killer. She stood in the cold, feeling the wind eat its way through her jacket like a ravenous animal. She zipped it up, but didn't feel any warmer.

"Are you going up again?" Angel shouted from the quad-chair line.

Will was beside Angel. Behind them stood Chris and Isabel.

"No," Kelly said, "not yet."

She looked at Will, who seemed restless, waiting for his ride to the top. Had he intentionally misled her? Had he pretended he was a cop, or had she just read into his words. All he'd said was, *If you're afraid, call me.* He'd never claimed to be with the police. She decided he was just trying to be nice.

Kelly sighed and hoped Shellborn and Troy solved their cases fast. If they didn't, Kelly was afraid she might never see Jeff again.

Jeff tried to stop thinking about Kelly. It was almost impossible. He had to find a way of getting her off his mind.

He took three runs down the Chute, by himself, going far faster than he should have for his first day on black diamond trails. After the third, he felt better, his head clearer, and he decided he could use some company, as long as it wasn't Kelly. He found two cute college girls and spent the afternoon teaching them how to steer their skis.

When they left they gave him their dorm phone number and invited him to come visit them some weekend on the University of Maryland campus.

"Sure," he said, trying to sound cheerful. "I'll give you a call." They were pretty and fun, but he missed Kelly already. He supposed he'd have to get used to that.

"Are you having a good time?" a voice sang out.

He spun around. "Angel, hi. Where are the others?" What he meant was, Where is Kelly?

She sighed. "All over the place. I can't seem to

keep track of everyone. It's so dangerous. There should be more of us to do a job like this." She moped a little, kicking at the snow with her white boots, her pale silvery hair floating about her face.

Here she goes again, Jeff thought. "Listen, Angel, how about you give that stuff a rest for a while and come ski with me. I could use the company."

Her lips drew into a pout. "I was sort of looking for Troy."

Jeff swore under his breath. What did this guy have that was so special?

"I have a feeling Troy's going to be busy for quite a while," he said.

She frowned. "Why?"

"I just think you'll have trouble getting anywhere with him, if you're considering him as a potential boyfriend."

"Really?"

"Really. Come on. Let's ski."

Just then he thought he saw something move, off to his right in the woods. He stopped and peered into the bank of thick-trunked trees but could see nothing. "Must be one of my guardian angels," he muttered.

16

By midnight everyone had gone to his or her bed, whether it was a real one with mattress and sheets, like Kelly's, or a pile of blankets heaped on rough wooden planks, where the boys had flopped down on the floor.

Kelly was so exhausted, she fell asleep almost as soon as she lay down. But something woke her up after what seemed only a few minutes.

She rolled over to peer at the glowing numerals on her travel alarm clock: 1:20 a.m. Closing her eyes firmly, she concentrated on wiping her mind free of the fears that dribbled through her brain, like steaming water dripping through coffee grounds—resulting only in muddy brown liquid. Muddy brown thoughts.

Troy was a cop. Someone had killed Paula and intended to frame her. Jeff hated her. Nothing else was clear. She blinked open her eyes, which stung with fatigue and tears. The clock read 1:50 a.m.

Groaning, Kelly turned onto her stomach and buried her damp cheeks in her pillow. But it did no good. She just couldn't sleep, and she couldn't puzzle her way out of the maze of conflicting clues.

Through the layers of pillow stuffing, Kelly felt subtle vibrations working their way up through the floor, the legs of her bed, her mattress, and into her body. Someone was out of bed, moving around inside the cabin. But it wasn't footsteps she heard. The sound was more like a muted rumble— growing louder then gradually softer.

Kelly sat up in bed, trying to identify the sound. The front door creaked softly, and she held her breath—listening . . . listening . . . The door latch clanked. The rumble was outside the cabin now, descending the ramp from the porch.

Kelly jumped out of bed and ran to the side window. All she could see were the shifting shadows of the woods in back of the cabin. Scrambling barefoot across the bedroom, she leapfrogged across the boys lying on the den floor and peered out the window beside the front door. In the dim light of a sliver of moon she glimpsed a figure in a wheelchair, bumping slowly along the path into the trees.

"Frank," she breathed. Where was he going at this time of night? He hated trying to maneuver his chair in the snow. Its awkwardness had kept him inside most of their stay at Wisp.

Kelly waited, watching the dark spaces between the tree trunks, vines, and boulders. Troy must be out there somewhere, keeping an eye on her as he'd promised. If he was, he'd see Frank leave and follow him, or make sure someone else tailed him.

But she saw nobody moving among the gnarled growth on either side of the path or on the path itself, nobody except Frank Riley, struggling to move his wheelchair over the frozen ground.

As quietly as possible, Kelly rushed back into her bedroom and pulled on jeans, a sweatshirt, heavy socks, and hiking boots. She grabbed her parka from the hook beside the front door.

As she silently slipped through the door, she cast a last look over her shoulder at Jeff, lying on his back on the floor, and had second thoughts about following Frank on her own. Should she wake him up and take him with her? No. He was still angry with her and would demand an explanation before agreeing to go.

There was no time for explanations. Frank would be out of sight in another minute or two.

Kelly ran down the ramp. Placing her feet carefully on the path, she avoided icy patches the resort's maintenance crew had missed when they'd sprinkled it with sand. She moved off in the direction she'd seen Frank taking.

Before the rains had come, washing away over a foot of snow, it would have been impossible for him to negotiate the paths in his chair. Although it was outfitted with ground-gripping rubber tires, the wooded walkways weren't shoveled, and the snow would have gripped the wheels, trapping him.

Now the slush resulting from the rain had frozen and been strewn with coarse, brown sand to make the connecting trails between cabins safe for walking.

Kelly could dimly see Frank up ahead, lurching and skidding over rough spots; he was making slow but steady progress.

She followed close enough to keep him in sight, but far enough back that he wouldn't hear the crunch of her step over the frozen ground.

At last, he stopped, seemed to hesitate, then looked around in the dark.

What is he up to? she wondered, her curiosity winning out over the warning voice that kept telling her to return to the cabin with the others, where she'd be safe. *What is he doing out here?*

Kelly ducked behind a wide pine tree off the left side of the path and held her breath, watching. Her heart hammered in her ears. Her upper lip beaded with droplets of sweat, although the air around her was well below freezing. She counted to ten before daring to peek around the gnarled bark of the tree to see what Frank was doing.

He'd stopped at one of the large wooden boxes where the maintenance crew stored sand for the paths. Casting one final look around the woods, he lifted the lid and reached inside.

Frank twisted his upper body and moved his arms and shoulders, trying to reach deeper into the box. But from his seated position, he could only get so far down.

"Come on!" Frank muttered. "Come on, I know you're in here!"

What is in there? Kelly thought. Was this what Troy had been waiting for? Was Frank Riley somehow involved in drug trafficking and was this a drop-off point for a shipment?

Kelly held her breath, unsure what to do.

Frank pounded his fist in frustration on the arm of his wheelchair. "There's got to be a way," he hissed.

Bracing his hands on either side of him, he shoved himself upwards, as if doing the seated pushups she'd seen him perform during his workouts at the cabin. He repeated the move three more times, finishing higher each time. On the last, he shoved himself forward, catching hold of the front edge of the wooden bin. He let out a grunt and slowly levered himself into a standing position, all of his weight carried by his stiffened arms.

Kelly was amazed at his strength. It was obvious his legs couldn't support him. She thought about what Shellborn had said about the knife thrust that had killed Paula, and shivered. *It had taken someone very strong to inflict it.* Kelly shivered again, recalling the night Frank had held Troy and Jeremy at knifepoint. The solution seemed so obvious.

Frank began to work quickly. Leaning over the

front of the box, he thrust one arm inside and sifted through the sand.

Where are you, Troy? Kelly thought wildly. *Come on, you can catch him with proof!*

Her heart raced, and her mind whirled with explanations that suddenly seemed so clear she couldn't understand why she hadn't understood what had happened before. It was like in chemistry class, stirring a reagent into a cloudy liquid—and suddenly the chemical reaction took place and the liquid cleared, as if by magic.

Frank had murdered Paula. She must have caught him with something incriminating, or doing something that would tip off the police that he was the one they were after. Kelly could imagine him panicking when he found out she was AWOL from a psychiatric hospital. No wonder he'd been angry with Annette for letting her stay. The police would come looking for her. And when they found her there was no telling what she'd say to them.

So he'd had to kill her.

Kelly's attention shifted back to Frank and the sand box.

If he got hold of whatever he'd stashed in the box and passed it along to whoever was buying it, the evidence would be lost.

All she could do was report to Shellborn or Troy what she'd seen. Frank could deny everything. It would be her word against his. And she'd learned a long time ago that when a kid and an adult told different stories, people usually believed the adult.

Impulsively, Kelly shot out through an opening in the bushes, streaking toward the box. She had to get to whatever Frank was after before he found it.

He must have seen her coming out of the corner of his eye. Wrenching his shoulders around, he demanded in a hoarse whisper, "What are you doing out here?"

"What about you?" Kelly asked. "Seems awful strange, you coming out here in the middle of the night for a couple of handfuls of sand."

He glared at her, but there was a shadow of fear behind his eyes. "Go back to the cabin right now," he growled.

Kelly stood her ground. "No."

"I said, get out of here. Get out before you get hurt."

"I'm not going to get hurt because I won't let you get close enough to me to do what you did to Paula."

He looked dumbfounded. "Paula?"

"How can you forget about her so fast?" she screamed, anger and sadness and hopelessness rising up inside of her, drowning out her fear. She'd read somewhere that people who kill often don't think of their victims as living human beings. Was that how Frank thought of Paula? Could he think that way about *her?*

"You believe I killed Paula?" he said, looking confused. He didn't give her a chance to answer. "You've got to get out of here—fast."

"I don't think so," Kelly said, reaching down into the sand. "Now let's see what you came after tonight."

Frank lunged for her across the wide wooden crate, but he couldn't reach her and still hold himself up. She kept one eye on his grappling fingers as she reached down . . . down, elbow deep in scratchy, damp granules.

"Don't!" he shouted. "You don't understand! I have to find—"

Kelly shut out his protests. She knew she was safe as long as she kept the sturdy bin between them. Reaching deeper, deeper still, she bent double over the waist-high wall. When the sand was nearly up to her shoulder, her fingertips ticked against something slick and hard.

Her eyes locked with Frank's. His expression was grim and knowing, as if he sensed she'd found what he'd been searching for.

"Give it to me. It's dangerous for you to have—"

"No way," she snapped back at him. He could bully Annette but she wouldn't let him do it to her.

Stretching out until she felt as if her body would break in two, Kelly grasped a corner of the object and tugged. It was heavy, much larger than she'd expected. Something wrapped tightly in plastic.

Her fingers closed around the lumpy shape and pulled it up through the sand. In the dark, she examined the package. Although it appeared to be encased in dark green plastic, like a garbage bag, she could still feel the outlines of the contents—a thin barrel, curved trigger guard, a molded grip . . . then more shapes of the same sort, all taped together in a bundle.

"Guns," she whispered.

"Yes, guns," a low voice sliced through the night air from behind her.

Kelly spun around to face Will Tanner, and relief flooded over her. "How did you know?" she asked. "I just found them. Frank must have hidden the guns in the sand box, or someone else stashed them there for him to pick up."

"How did I know?" Will chuckled, his face shifting eerily in the moon's silver wash. "I know because my friends put them there."

Kelly was confused. "What are you talking about?"

Will nodded toward Annette's husband. "Frank understands. Don't you, Frank? Why not tell her?"

"No!" Frank blurted out. "She doesn't have to know anything more. Let her go." He stared beseechingly at Kelly. "Run back to the cabin now. Run! Wake up the boys and tell them to go for help!"

Kelly only hesitated a second, but it was long enough for Will to pull a small revolver from his jacket pocket. "You're not going anywhere," he muttered.

He had always seemed so handsome, but now his eyes were dark and sinister, his smile was gone, and there was a heartless twist to his mouth.

"The guns belong to you?" Kelly asked, still clutching the bundle to her chest.

"Let's just say, I'm a small link in a very complicated chain. For the time being, they're mine."

"I saw him out here," Frank explained. "He was messing around in the sand early yesterday morning. I thought he might have booze or drugs stashed out here, but that didn't make sense. Nathan, I could see. But it was obvious Will wasn't into heavy drinking or drugs."

"The parties," Kelly murmured, her mind whirling suddenly into gear. "You weren't going for the fun of it, like everyone else. It was a job, wasn't it? You left early with a girl and drove around, picking up guns and delivering them. If you got stopped by a cop, it would look like you were just having a good time driving around with your girlfriend."

Frank nodded. "Annette said he was just popular. I told her there was more to him than that. She thought I was imagining things."

So that was what they'd been arguing about, at least part of the time.

"You sell guns to kids!" Kelly accused him.

"Don't push for any more information," Frank warned her. "The less we know the better our chances." His eyes met Will's. "Let her go. You can pick up your shipment and disappear. You don't have to kill her."

Kelly winced. Would Will do that? Murder her?

The answer flickered through her mind, like letters in an advertisement flickering across an electric scoreboard.

Of course he would. He'd killed Paula, hadn't he?

What had she found in the boys' bedroom? A gun? Like the one he carried now, which was aimed at her chest?

"The parties you went to . . ." Kelly murmured. "I'll bet they were all along I-95. From there you could drive a hundred miles or more in a night easily, all up and down the East Coast. The girls probably never knew what you were doing."

"Washington, Newark, New Jersey, even as far away as New York City . . ." Will looked delighted with himself. "I could do any of them in one night. My parents thought I was spending the night at a friend's house after the party. Told them I didn't want to wake them up, coming in late." Will grinned, looking pleased with himself. "It was easy money, and lots of it."

"Some of those guns show up in schools," Frank said. "Some end up in the hands of gangs who shoot it out in the streets of Baltimore or D.C. Innocent little kids get killed in the crossfire." Kelly could see the pain in his eyes. He really did care.

"Hey," Will said, flipping the gun in his hand, "what happens after they leave my hands ain't my problem. It's just business. But I do have other problems. *She* is one of them, you're the other." He turned to Kelly. "You, move over closer to Mr. Has-Been Ski Champ."

She saw Frank's arms tense. The knuckles in his hands grew white as he clutched the bin. She wasn't sure what Will had planned for her, but she didn't want to make things any easier on him. Kelly didn't move.

"I said, *move it!*" he growled, waving the gun in her direction.

"What are you going to do, Will, shoot us both?" Frank asked. He looked as if he was tiring of holding himself up. His arms started shaking, and his face was flushed with exertion.

"Two more murders will give the police plenty of clues to work on," Kelly added. "Someone will hear the shots. They'll figure out it was you. You don't want to spend the rest of your life in jail, do you?" Kelly asked breathlessly.

"And your bosses won't like your jeopardizing their business any more than you already have," Frank pointed out.

"My employers don't need to worry," Will laughed. "The cops won't be looking for me. As far as they'll know, Kelly stumbled on you while you were checking on your illegal firearms shipment. Hey, everyone's seen you zipping all over in that nifty, specially-equipped Jeep of yours. You could have been running guns and she found out."

Kelly felt her blood run cold. There was something different about the way Will was looking at her, almost as if she weren't there, had never been there. Will was going to kill them both—she could feel it.

She thought sadly about Annette. The young teacher would be told her dead husband had been a criminal . . . when what he'd really tried to do was save the lives of a lot of innocent people, including her student.

She thought about her father. He'd hear the news from Shellborn, who had been calling him four times a day to reassure him that everything was under control.

Nothing was under control. The world was about to explode with a couple of pulls on a trigger.

"It won't work, Will," Frank said tightly.

"Oh, I think it will. It will look as if you, Frank, came after Kelly with a knife. This one," he said, pulling a kitchen knife from inside his jacket. "See? This might even be the one you waved around when those two boys broke into the cabin. You flipped out again, stabbed her. But before she died, well . . . she must have grabbed one of your guns, one that was loaded, and blasted you. Some very upset skier will find two bodies lying in the snow come morning. Or maybe I'll discover you myself, and run to the nearest phone to report the tragedy." He shook his head with mock regret.

Kelly took a step away from the box.

"I wouldn't try to run," Will warned her. "If I have to shoot you first, it will make things a little more complicated for me, but you'll be just as dead."

Kelly stared into the depths of his eyes and knew he meant every word he'd said.

17

In the moonlight, from the window of his own cabin, Troy could see the dim outline of Kelly's cabin and five or six others nestled in the woods. Everything was quiet now. No one walked through the woods. He looked at his watch; it was almost midnight.

More than luck had landed him with a good view of several of the cabins in the area, including the one the Thomaston High kids had rented. He'd researched the layout of the resort weeks before spring break. The lieutenant had arranged for the rental agent to give Troy's group a cabin with central location.

He sat at the window, sipping black coffee, watching, waiting. Soon, something would happen . . . *had to happen* if they were going to catch that girl's killer. Troy ached for a chance to finally spring into action after so many tedious days and nights of doing nothing but wait.

As the minutes slid past, he started feeling a little lightheaded, but not really tired. He was past exhaustion; he'd allowed himself only a few hours of sleep during the middle of each day when he was sure the risk would be too high for a drug trafficker or a killer to make a move. He felt as if he were leaving his own body and floating above his chair to observe himself as he gazed out the window at the snowy woods.

From his hovering vantage point, he was able to take in all of the woods below, with the cabins spread out in a tidy pattern, like tiny buildings in the make-believe village his mother always set up beneath their Christmas tree. He thought to himself how wonderful it was to be able to do his job like this, seeing everything in the resort spread out before him in such clear detail, as if it was a map.

"Hey! You going to sit there all night *again?*" someone demanded.

Troy jumped. His eyes flashed open, and he looked up in shock at Jeremy.

"What?"

"You do this every night, Troy. Sit there, staring out the window. I don't know what you find so interesting," Jeremy said with a deep sigh. "I just got up to make myself some hot chocolate since I couldn't sleep. But you're having no trouble."

Troy shot up out of his chair, grabbed Jeremy by the shoulders of his flannel pajamas and shook him. "What are you talking about?"

Jeremy's eyes bulged behind the thick lenses of his eye glasses. "You been asleep for over an hour."

Troy stared at his watch and felt his pulse shoot up. It was almost 2 a.m. With his heart in his throat he swung around to face the window. There were no lights on in the Thomaston High cabin. Nothing appeared to be moving. But what might have happened while he was dozing?

Troy seized his jacket from the back of his chair.

"Where are you going?" Jeremy whined. "Mrs. Cornwall said no one leaves after curfew."

"Out of my way!" Troy roared, pushing past the boy.

"You sure can be rude sometimes," Jeremy called after him.

Troy slammed through the front door, vaulted off the steps, and cut through the tangle of winter-dead brush, straight for Kelly's cabin. An aching feeling in his gut told him as he ran that he'd missed something important.

He might have blown his very first case!

Worse yet, something might have happened to Kelly while he was supposed to be protecting her.

Only the other day, he'd learned from the two detectives covering telephone surveillance on the lodge phones that some kind of delivery had been arranged between a man at Wisp and another in Tennessee. What was in the shipment, the wire tap guys didn't know. But if the shipment were drugs, they could be packed in one of the students' luggage and transported safely back to Thomaston in the bus.

Troy had already searched all of the cabins in the area, but he'd come up with nothing. He'd have liked to bring in a drug dog and handler, but that would tip off the bad guys.

Troy stopped short of the cabin, breathing hard, warily studying the dark windows. He slowly circled around to the window of the boys' bedroom and pulled a compact flashlight from his coat pocket. Shining it through the glass, he peered into the room but saw no one.

He moved silently to the girls' room. Inside, he could see Angel in her bed. Isabel too. Kelly's bed was empty.

A scratchy knot worked its way up through his chest and into his throat as if a frightened little animal was trying to fight its way out of a collapsed burrow. Troy ran around to the front of the cabin. He had to find out if everyone was accounted for. Kelly, like Jeremy, might just have gotten up for a late-night snack.

The front door wasn't locked. *Bad sign,* he thought. Annette or Frank would have bolted up for the night. Slowly, he eased up the metal latch on the cabin door and pushed inward. The door swung open.

Troy slipped inside the dark den and turned to shut the door to prevent the cold draft from waking the boys. He took one step forward, but before he could get any further, an arm locked around his throat, cutting off his breath.

"Let go!" Troy gasped, using the last air in his lungs.

"What are you doing here?"

Troy didn't have the time or patience to explain. In one practiced move, he bent forward while jabbing an elbow into his attacker's stomach. He heard a shocked grunt, then reached up over and behind his head. Grabbing a handful of hair, Troy dropped to one knee, and flipped the guy over and onto his back with a loud thud.

Everything happened at once then.

Someone hit the lights. Chris leaped up from his sleeping bag on the floor. Angel poked her head around the corner from her bedroom door. Isabel ran past her into the den, knocking over a lamp that crashed to the floor.

"Oh good, we're having a party!" Angel cried, her eyes sparkling as she took in Troy wrestling on the floor with Jeff.

Annette lunged through her bedroom door, clutching her bathrobe around her. "What's going on here? Frank! Frank, where are you?"

Troy didn't dare take his eyes off of Jeff, who he'd finally pinned to the floor by wedging one knee into the middle of his back. He kept a steady pressure on the arm he'd twisted behind Jeff.

"Sorry, Mrs. Riley," Troy said. "I don't have a lot of time to explain. I need to know who's missing. Is Kelly here?"

Annette gave him her best enraged-teacher-about-to-send-student-to-the-office glare. "Let that boy up this instance! This is the second time you've broken in here. I'm reporting you to the po—" She blinked at the badge Troy was holding up. "Oh, you *are* the police?" she finished meekly.

"Yes, ma'am. I'm sorry, but I need to know who has left the cabin. This is an emergency."

"Let me up," Jeff grunted. "Kelly's not here. I was looking for her when you showed up. We have to find her."

"*You* aren't going anywhere," Troy said, at last releasing his grip on Jeff's wrist. "I'll find her. Now, who else isn't here?"

"Nathan's in the bathroom," Angel said helpfully. "He's sick. I think he got some liquor from a boy in another cabin. He's been throwing up all night."

"Good. What about your husband?" Troy asked, turning back to Annette. "Where is he?"

"I-I don't know," Annette stammered, her eyes spreading out flat and dull with worry. "I didn't hear him leave the bedroom."

Jeff rubbed the back of his neck. "Will wasn't here when I woke up."

"Will, Frank, and Kelly," Troy repeated. "And no one has any idea where any of them went?"

Four heads shook, side to side.

Troy swiveled around toward the door.

"She was telling the truth, wasn't she?" Jeff asked.

"If you mean when Kelly told you she wasn't interested in me as a boyfriend—yeah. I made her promise she wouldn't tell anyone who I was." He reached for the latch, then had another thought. "Someone go to my cabin and call 911. Jeremy's awake and will let you in."

"What do we say?" Angel asked, beaming at him like a three-way light bulb on high.

"Tell them Chase needs a backup, pronto."

Troy had run no further than a hundred yards into the woods when Jeff overtook him. "Go back!" Troy snapped.

"You might need help," Jeff gasped. "Two guys against one isn't great odds."

"I have a feeling Will Tanner's the one to watch out for," Troy said.

"What's he done?"

"Dealing or transporting drugs, maybe. I'm not sure yet, but it doesn't look good."

"Is he dangerous?"

"He is if he's the one who killed that girl," Troy said.

Jeff looked pale in the faint light of the moon reflected off the snow. Troy knew he was thinking about Kelly.

He stopped running and held out a hand to signal Jeff to stop too, then pulled him down behind a boulder.

"What is it?" Jeff whispered.

"It's them. Over there by that storage thing."

Jeff stared at the three figures surrounding the wooden container. "What are you waiting for? He's holding a gun on Kelly."

"He'll kill her if we don't do this right," Troy muttered. His mind jerked itself from one option to another. Why couldn't he think straight? How long before his backup arrived?

The two of them could rush Will, maybe knock the gun out of his hand. But they were far enough away that Will would get off at least one shot. The first would be for Kelly.

He could retreat with Jeff, without letting Will see them, and wait for Shellborn and Baxter to show up. But if Will intended to kill Kelly and Frank, he might do it before cops with more experience than he had time to reach them.

Troy didn't know what to do. This had started

out an easy first case, just get information about some high school kids who might be selling drugs. And now look at what was happening. He already had one body on his hands.

In another minute, it might be three, or more.

Kelly looked at Frank across the sand bin. There was something different about him. Something in the intense way he was looking at her and the rigid position of his body, propped on the edge of the bin. It was almost as if he felt in charge of the situation, although he was facing a loaded gun.

"Move closer to Frank," Will ordered.

"Do what he says, Kelly," Frank said softly when she didn't move. "We don't want to make him any madder than he is."

"But he's going to *kill* us!" she cried.

Will grinned. "Hey, it's finally sinking in."

"If you won't let the girl go," Frank said, "at least make it quick. Don't play around at it."

Kelly couldn't believe what she was hearing. *Make it quick?*

"Come on, *move it!*" Will barked, waving the knife at her with one hand while he kept the pistol aimed at Frank.

She sidled around the box, hoping something, anything would happen to buy her some time. Troy had to be around somewhere. Wouldn't he realize she and Will were missing? What about Annette? If she woke up to find Frank wasn't in the cabin but the Jeep was still there, she'd know something was wrong.

Kelly kept moving slowly, inching closer to Frank. When they were standing side by side, Will seemed satisfied.

"Good. Now I'll honor your request, Frank."

His smile dissolving from his lips, Will stepped around the corner of the box and lunged at Kelly, the knife blade flashing toward her. At the same moment, Frank released his grip on the wooden bin and threw himself into Will's path, his whole body tumbling forward.

Kelly screamed and tripped over Frank's legs, landing in the snow. She scrambled to her feet, looking on in horror as the knife's blade slashed at Frank's plaid shirt, ripping through the cloth. He crashed down onto the snow, blood seeping out of him.

"Run, Kelly!" he gasped. "Run!"

Her heart hammering wildly in her chest, she tore through the trees . . . straight into Jeff's arms. He held onto her tightly, pulling her off the path and to the ground.

Troy dashed past them, his face screwed up with determination. Leaping into the air, he hurtled toward Will.

"No!" Kelly screamed as she saw Will swing around and aim the gun at the young police officer.

Her eyes fixed on the knife Will had dropped. Breaking free from Jeff, she grabbed the knife from where it lay on the ground.

Kelly had no sense of how to hold or throw the weapon. She simply hurled it at Will—and it flew through the air, twisting in a floppy, slow-motion arc.

Will must have seen it coming out of the corner of his eye. He whipped around in the same second he squeezed the trigger. The shot flew wild, missing Troy. Without taking time to aim, he pulled the trigger a second time, and the bullet struck his own foot.

Will's yowl of pain turned into a dull *umph* when Troy tackled him, knocking him into a pile of leaves. In the next instant Troy and Jeff had pinned him to the ground.

Kelly stood shakily, adrenaline pumping . . .

pumping . . . pumping through her veins as if some invisible motor inside of her refused to turn off.

Suddenly, the clearing seemed crowded with people. Angel and Annette burst through the trees with Chris and Nathan close behind them. Isabel popped out of the woods from the opposite direction, with Jeremy tripping along behind her.

"Ow!" Will shrieked, writhing on the ground, trying to get a look at his injured foot. "Get me a doctor! I've been shot! Can't you see I'm shot?"

"Shut up," Troy gasped. "It's just a scratch."

Annette rushed to Frank and dropped on her knees beside him. Pressing her hand over the bloody patch of cloth over his chest, she wept and whispered soft things to him.

"He saved my life," Kelly choked out. "He threw himself between me and Will even though he knew he couldn't get up and protect himself."

Annette's tears dropped on her young husband's cheek as she lovingly stroked the mussed hair back from his forehead. His eyes were open, blinking at her, but he didn't seem capable of talking.

"The police and an ambulance are on the way," Isabel said. "I just called them from Jeremy's cabin."

Kelly buried her face in Jeff's shoulder, unable to watch any longer.

"Hold on, Frank . . . just a little longer. Hold on," Annette pleaded.

18

"What's taking him so long?" Kelly fumed. She paced alongside her father's car, anxious to start the trip home to Thomaston.

"Give him some slack, will ya?" Jeff called down from the top where he was clamping their skis into the roof-rack. "He's talking to Shellborn."

"He's been in there for almost an hour," she said, tossing the cabin a curious look. "They settled all the official police business yesterday, I thought. What can they have to talk about now?"

Angel and Troy stepped through the front door and onto the porch. They were holding hands, and Angel was gazing dreamily up into Troy's eyes as he talked, taking in every word as if it were the last anyone would ever speak to her.

"Man, is he in for trouble," Jeff commented under his breath.

Kelly laughed. "I think Officer Chase, of all people, can take care of himself."

"I guess."

"I wonder if he'll take her to the prom in June."

"An undercover cop at our prom." Jeff moved the words around in his mouth as if they tasted bad then jumped down to the ground.

"Probably wouldn't be the first time," Kelly remarked.

With all the trouble about drugs and underage

drinking and fights at dances, the police were usually around anyway.

It made her sad, thinking about how going to school had changed since she was a little kid in elementary school. There had been no need for the police then. Even in middle school, she'd been unaware of crime and was never afraid of taking a back stairway or staying late to work on a project. Things were different now. Worse, much worse. And it had happened because people had made it happen.

Just like Paula had caused Brian's death, even though she hadn't planned it, and Will had killed Paula because he didn't want anyone to find out he was transporting guns illegally, and he was so greedy he didn't want to give up the money he was being paid.

The door opened again, and Nathan, Chris, and Isabel dragged their suitcases out onto the porch and down the wheelchair ramp.

"Did you hear?" Isabel asked, setting her suitcase on the snowy ground beside the Rileys' Jeep.

"Hear what?" Kelly asked.

"Annette told Shellborn that Frank is off the critical list. He's been moved into a regular room in the hospital. He's going to be okay!"

Kelly grinned. "That's the first good news I've heard all day."

"No, it's not," Jeff reminded her, "the first was this morning when the police said we could all go home."

Instead of returning her students to Thomaston by bus, Annette had decided it would make more sense for them to ride in private cars since most of them wanted to do that anyway. She would stay at Wisp so that she could be near Frank while he recovered from the surgery to close the knife wound.

Kelly's dad had arrived the previous night and planned to take Kelly and Jeff home with him as soon as the police finished their investigation. There was room in the car for two more, so Isabel and Chris would ride with them. Troy's cover had been blown by his obvious role in capturing Will, so there was no point to his remaining with the school group he'd arrived with. He had his own car, and he planned to drive Angel back to Thomaston. He'd offered to give Nathan a lift, but Angel's old boyfriend had other plans.

"I'm not going back," he'd told them the night before. "Not ever."

"What are you talking about?" Chris asked. "That's crazy. That's where your home is."

"No," Nathan said, solemnly. "Crazy is hanging around my father and old friends any longer—not you guys, I mean the others."

Kelly knew exactly who he was talking about. Nathan's friends spent their weekends drinking and breaking into houses and smashing up anything that struck them as fun to destroy. And the only difference between them and his father was the old man didn't break things unless he stumbled over them when he was drunk.

"What will you do?" she asked him.

He shrugged. "For starters, maybe I'll stay off the booze for a while and see what things look like sober. I mean, you guys just about forced me to give it up anyway."

"Good," Isabel said. "You can do it."

"How about school?" Jeff asked.

"Oh, I don't know." Nathan looked away into the fire. "I've never been very good at that. I'll get my GED sometime. Maybe I'll try something else for awhile, like working at one of the ski boat rentals. They open in another month or so. A guy I met at the lodge said they're already looking for pre-

185

season help to clean up equipment. I'll bet I could find a cabin to share with a couple of other guys."

"We'll miss you, Nathan," Kelly said, touching him on the arm.

He smiled sadly. "No, you won't. But thanks for saying it anyway."

Kelly's thoughts returned to the present as her father and Shellborn stepped out of the cabin. She watched them with interest as they lingered on the porch.

The lady cop had arrived that morning in off-duty clothes—jeans, a pretty pastel blouse, and athletic shoes that looked a lot like the ones Kelly wore. Shellborn let loose one of her sunny smiles, directing it up at Frank Peterson.

Kelly frowned.

"What's wrong now?" Jeff asked, wrapping an arm around her waist. He kissed the red waves on top of her head.

"Look at them," she groaned. "They're acting like two kids meeting for the first time at a dance. It's totally embarrassing."

Her father said something to Shellborn, and she threw back her head and laughed, blushing.

Jeff chuckled. "Your dad seems awfully interested in her. I thought you said he doesn't date."

"He doesn't . . . at least, he hasn't that I know of." It occurred to her that there might be other things she didn't know about her father. Like what he and Shellborn had talked about all those times she'd called to update him on the investigation and how Kelly was faring. After a while, maybe they hadn't talked about her at all. Maybe a five-minute call to reassure him had turned into an hour-long visit.

Isabel stretched up on tiptoes to whisper in her ear. "Have you ever thought about having a new mom?"

Kelly stared at her, shocked.

Isabel's dark eyes glittered with mischief then grew serious again. "She's awful nice, Kel. She got you eating again, and she's sure a lot of fun to be around. Imagine having a cop for a mother."

Kelly stared at her hands and wondered how she'd feel about that. Not that it would ever happen . . . not that Dad would finally get over his wife ditching him and find someone really nice who deserved him as much as he deserved her. Someone who liked jigsaw puzzles, talking about girl things, and told her to eat her food because she'd paid for it and she wasn't going to throw it away.

Slowly a smile crept across Kelly's lips, and she looked at Isabel, then at Jeff.

"You know, that might not be bad at all."

SPINE-TINGLING SUSPENSE FROM AVON FLARE

NICOLE DAVIDSON

THE STALKER	76645-0/ $3.50 US/ $4.50 Can
CRASH COURSE	75964-0/ $3.99 US/ $4.99 Can
WINTERKILL	75965-9/ $3.99 US/ $4.99 Can
DEMON'S BEACH	76644-2/ $3.50 US/ $4.25 Can
FAN MAIL	76995-6/ $3.50 US/ $4.50 Can
SURPRISE PARTY	76996-4/ $3.50 US/ $4.50 Can
NIGHT TERRORS	72243-7/ $3.99 US/ $4.99 Can

THE BAND by Carmen Adams	77328-7/ $3.99 US/ $4.99 Can
EVIL IN THE ATTIC by Linda Piazza	77576-X/ $3.99 US/ $4.99 Can
BACK FROM THE DEAD by Carol Gorman	77433-X/ $3.99 US/ $4.99 Can
THE LAST LULLABY by Jesse Osburn	77317-1/ $3.99 US/ $4.99 Can